Dangerous Deceits

Dangerous
Deceits

Cherith Baldry

Cherith Baldry

Matador
9 Priory Business Park,
Wistow Road, Kibworth Beauchamp,
Leicestershire. LE8 0RX
Tel: 0116 279 2299
Email: books@troubador.co.uk
Web: www.troubador.co.uk/matador
Twitter: @matadorbooks

ISBN 978 1789016 154

British Library Cataloguing in Publication Data.
A catalogue record for this book is available from the British Library.

Typeset in 11pt Minion Pro by Troubador Publishing Ltd, Leicester, UK
Printed and bound by CPI Group (UK) Ltd, Croydon, CR0 4YY

Matador is an imprint of Troubador Publishing Ltd

In memory of Peter Baldry
1947–1999

...blasphemous fables and dangerous deceits.
The Book of Common Prayer, Article xxxi

All the quotations at the chapter headings are taken from
the Book of Common Prayer, 1662

Chapter One

Man that is born of a woman hath but a short time to live...
The Order for the Burial of the Dead

The telephone rang. Gawaine St Clair, acting on the assumption that no one who knew him would call him so early and that therefore it must be a wrong number, ignored it. It went on ringing. Finally, exasperated, he uncurled himself from his corner of the couch, padded into the hall, taking his coffee with him, and picked up the receiver.

"Gawaine?"

He winced. "Christabel," he murmured. "How delightful."

Gawaine had grown up addressing his present caller as 'Aunt Christabel', on the rather dubious grounds that she had been at school with his mother. He had, as he was fond of pointing out, no living relatives closer than a third cousin. However, Christabel Cottesmore had retained the auntly habit of calling on him for those little services which her own children could not render, having wisely scattered to various remote corners of the globe as soon as it was practicable to do so. Gawaine, living little more than ten miles away, was easy prey.

As on this occasion.

1

"I want you to take me to Guildford to look at a body."

It was not, Gawaine reflected, April the First. Perhaps there was some autumnal Feast of Fools which he had unaccountably failed to register.

"Certainly," he replied. "Have you a particular body in mind?"

Christabel's snort nearly blew the receiver apart. "Don't be more of an idiot than you can help, Gawaine. It's the vicar's body – at least, the police think it is."

For the first time, and with the help of another mouthful of coffee, the conversation began to make sense to Gawaine. Two weeks before, the vicar of St Paul's, Christabel's parish church, had disappeared, under what are normally referred to as mysterious circumstances, from the priest's vestry just before the nine-fifteen Communion service. Christabel had made a determined attempt to persuade Gawaine to investigate the disappearance, but he had firmly refused, on the grounds that if the vicar had wished to abscond it was his own business.

Christabel, on her authority as Vicar's Warden, had reported the matter to the police, and Gawaine had to admit she had been justified, since if this was indeed the vicar's body, he had presumably not absconded of his own free will.

"Has he no family to identify him?" he asked.

"I think there's a brother somewhere." Gawaine could see Christabel's shrug as clearly as if she was standing in front of him. "But I gather the police haven't managed to track him down. Now, how soon can you get here?"

"I thought the police would send a car for you," Gawaine suggested cautiously, playing for time.

"Oh, they offered, but I knew you would drive me. After all, you'll be coming into it now, won't you?"

Gawaine closed his eyes and hugged the receiver. The last thing he wanted was to be involved with murder, again, but he could see, with the awful inevitability of Greek tragedy, that he would indeed be coming into it.

He was aware of Christabel's voice, the strident tones muffled but still audible, and lifted the receiver again to the vicinity of his ear.

"What's the matter with you?" Christabel was complaining. "Have you gone to sleep?"

"I might well," Gawaine returned edgily, "if you will ring up when dawn is cracking."

"It's half past ten in the morning!"

"Precisely."

Gawaine finished his coffee and hummed the theme of a Bach partita while Christabel gave him a detailed summary of his habits (unsatisfactory), morals (about which she didn't dare to think), antecedents (better than he deserved), and duties (unfulfilled), and ended by asking again when he would pick her up.

"An hour," he promised, and put down the receiver before she could ask why it would take him an hour to drive ten miles.

Slightly more than an hour later, showered, dressed and just about fully conscious, Gawaine pulled into the drive of Christabel's stockbroker Tudor residence. Her husband, the aforementioned stockbroker, had long since fled to his lair in the City, but Christabel's Golf was parked in front of the house. Gawaine wondered, not for the first time, why Christabel was so insistent on having his company. She could hardly wish for moral support – certainly not from him – and looking at a whole battlefield of dead bodies was hardly likely to affect her driving. Gawaine came to the conclusion that it was all a ploy, part of her campaign to get him to investigate, and he acknowledged with a faint sigh that it had probably worked.

He was putting on the handbrake when Christabel bounced out of the front door. She was a tall woman, in her fifties, vigorous and not totally unattractive. As usual she was aggressively well-groomed, and wore a charcoal grey suit, clearly chosen as an appropriate garment for the viewing of bodies.

"I don't understand," she said as Gawaine held open the passenger door for her, "why you don't change your car. You can afford to drive something better than this heap."

Since the heap, although modest, was a mere three years old, Gawaine thought this was rather unfair. "I like this car," he answered mildly as he got back in and started the engine.

This time he had to face Christabel's snort unprotected by several miles of British Telecom cable. He suppressed a sigh. It was going to be a long drive.

Measured in miles, the journey to Guildford was a short one, but in Christabel's company crossing the street could seem like a world tour. Gawaine filtered out what facts he could learn from the rest of her conversation. The body that waited for them had been discovered by walkers on the Downs the day before, and had come from there into the jurisdiction of the Guildford police. It had been, Christabel told him, dead for about a fortnight.

4

"So if it is your vicar," Gawaine mused, "he must have been killed fairly soon after he disappeared."

This remark was a tacit admission that he had accepted his fate, and Christabel, with a nod of triumph, recognised it as such.

"If he's been dead a fortnight," Gawaine went on, "won't he…well, will there be very much left to identify?"

"Since the police have called me to identify him," Christabel retorted magisterially, "it is presumably possible to do so. One must be strong-minded about these things."

Gawaine made no comment and tried not to feel sick.

They were delayed on the outskirts of Guildford while Gawaine tried to find his way. Christabel's directions consisted of yelling, "Go left!" when left was clearly marked No Entry, and this habit, coupled with Gawaine's inability to work out which side of a map was the top, meant that they drove twice round the cathedral and once through the purlieus of the university before they reached their destination.

"You need a satnav," Christabel informed him.

So far Gawaine had resisted handing over control of his journeys to an electronic device, but he reflected that being harangued by a disembodied voice might be preferable to being harangued by Christabel. "You could be right," he murmured.

Once arrived, Gawaine was profoundly relieved when Christabel refused his tentative offer to accompany her inside, and Christabel, after a few well-chosen remarks about pusillanimity and lack of moral fibre, with which Gawaine agreed absolutely, left him sitting in the car.

Alone at last, he tried without success to direct his mind towards something aesthetically more pleasing, but it stubbornly refused to be dragged away from the problem of why the incumbent of St Paul's should vanish from his vestry and be subsequently discovered decomposing in a thicket on the North Downs. What could have made him abandon his congregation without a word to anyone to explain where he was going and why?

Gawaine had never met the vicar, he could not be expected to account for what had happened to him, but that unfortunately did not prevent the problem from nagging at him. It did not prevent, either, his imagining uncomfortably what Christabel had gone to face, and he felt he should have insisted on going with her.

His train of thought was interrupted by a sudden movement beside the car. The passenger door opened and someone got in. Gawaine started. Not Christabel. Definitely not Christabel. He took in the glossy chestnut hair, the amused expression, and, flinching inwardly, the reporter's notebook and pencil.

"Miss Brown," he said politely.

"Ms."

Gawaine looked inquiring. "How do you pronounce that?"

"You just heard me pronounce it, for goodness' sake!" Persephone Brown snapped open her notebook. "In any case, don't try to side-track me. The missing vicar, St Paul's, Ellingwood. Yes? Whodunit, Gawaine?"

Gawaine took a breath. His previous acquaintance with Seff Brown had left him with an unquestioning respect for her intelligence but this was the first time he had ever thought she might have second sight as well.

"My dear Persephone…" he began in his best languid manner.

"Come off it, Gawaine. Look. A man disappears. A body turns up. You also turn up. And you live…what… about ten miles from Ellingwood? The only thing I can't explain is why you're out here in the car park, instead of inside, conferring with the cops."

"I have no official standing," Gawaine replied austerely.

"When do you ever? Come on, Gawaine. Give."

For some reason that he did not care to formulate, Gawaine felt he would prefer it if Seff had disappeared before Christabel returned. And telling her something would be the quickest – indeed the only – way of getting rid of her. Besides, she was wearing culottes and a top in a hot Javanese print that he privately felt was rather fierce, and clashed with the upholstery of the car.

"I brought someone," he explained. "A friend – one of the churchwardens – to see if she could identify the body."

Seff scribbled. "Tell me about his disappearance," she said.

"You probably know more about it than I do."

Seff flashed him a look. "I know he was seen in the vestry a few minutes before the nine-fifteen service, and then when it was time for the service to start, he'd gone. Leaving the lay reader to take Matins."

"Then you do know more than I do, my dear Persephone. No one told me about the lay reader."

Gawaine was aware that Seff was measuring him up. She knew – or he hoped she knew – that he would not tell her a direct lie.

To his relief, after a minute she nodded slightly. "Fair enough. Now we'll just have to wait for your friend to come back, won't we?"

This time Gawaine's flinching was not inward.

Seff gave him a wicked grin. "Don't worry, Gawaine," she assured him. "Just remember my bedside manner."

That was the trouble. On the track of a story, Seff had all the bedside manner of a meat cleaver. The clash of mighty opposites would be a mild way of describing her encounter with Christabel. And Gawaine could hardly eject her from his car. There was no sign of Christabel yet, but how long did it take to identify a body?

"Really…" he began fretfully.

"Are you going to be in on this?" Seff asked. Clearly she was intent on improving the shining hour while she waited.

Gawaine shrugged. "I expect so."

The look Seff gave him was suddenly more sympathetic. "You don't enjoy it, do you?"

"No, but I don't think I have much choice."

"So why don't you give David a ring?"

Seff had given voice to a thought which had been creeping around the back of Gawaine's own mind, which so far he had been able to ignore.

"No, I don't think so," he replied. "Fearful imposition, don't you think?"

"The point, surely, is what he thinks?"

Gawaine shrugged again, and found nothing to say to that. Staring through the windscreen, he saw that Christabel had just emerged. He stiffened slightly.

"There she is!" Seff exclaimed.

"How do you know?"

"You just told me," Seff said smugly. "Besides, you leapt about six inches when she appeared. Don't worry, I'll go and grab her over there. Listen – if I have to come to Ellingwood, can I scrounge a bed with you?"

"Unchaperoned?" Gawaine inquired primly.

Seff laughed and blew him a kiss as she got out of the car. Gawaine watched as she dodged between parked cars and intercepted Christabel, who was steaming across in his direction. He shuddered slightly and closed his eyes. The meeting was mercifully out of earshot, and he much preferred it to be out of sight as well.

Chapter Two

...such men as are given to change, and have always discovered a greater regard to their own private fancies and interests, than to that duty they owe to the publick.

Preface to the Book of Common Prayer

"Did you have that woman in here?" Christabel asked accusingly, as if she suspected Gawaine of having a whole harem.

"Yes, she was asking about your vicar. We've met before."

Gawaine closed the car door on Christabel and missed her reply as he went round to the driver's seat.

"Impertinence!" was the next word that he caught, though whether it referred to himself or Seff he wasn't sure.

"Was it the vicar?" he asked.

Christabel nodded. She had an expression of frozen-faced disapproval, as if the cat had made a mess on her drawing room rug.

"Murdered?"

"Of course murdered. Hit over the head. Honestly, Gawaine, if all you can do is ask fool questions..."

She subsided to a slow simmer. Gawaine recognised that his last chance of remaining uncommitted had just vanished.

10

"We need to talk," Christabel announced as he started the car. "We'd better stop somewhere for lunch on the way back. It's getting awfully late."

Gawaine threaded his way out of the city – with rather more skill than he had shown while threading his way in – and pulled up not much later in the forecourt of a country hotel he had visited before. He reflected that he might as well be sure of a good lunch, since he was fairly certain about who would be picking up the tab.

"It might do," Christabel said, looking around her disagreeably.

She led the way into the dining room, which at this time was almost empty. A waitress bustled over to them and settled them at a table in a bay window, which overlooked a little courtyard crowded with tubs of scarlet geraniums, and a ginger cat asleep in the sun. Very pleasant, Gawaine thought, regretting that he would not be left to contemplate the prospect in peace.

Christabel ordered salmon and a half bottle of Chardonnay. "Since," she said, "you're driving, Gawaine. Why not try one of those alcohol free lagers?"

Gawaine shuddered, and asked for Perrier. "Tell me about your vicar," he suggested.

"He wasn't our vicar."

Before Gawaine could react to this apparently nonsensical remark, Christabel went on to explain that St Paul's was at present undergoing an interregnum. The previous vicar had been called to higher things – not heaven, but a retirement cottage on the South Downs – at the beginning of the summer, and owing to the peculiar laws and customs of the Anglican Church, at least three months had to elapse before another vicar could replace him. In fact, the interregnum had lasted for more than four months now, and the parish was just getting ready to advertise the vacancy.

"And that was another problem with Father Thomas," Christabel said, betraying unchristian animosity.

"Father Thomas being the body?" Gawaine inquired.

"Yes. Thomas Coates, his name was, but he liked to be called Father Thomas. Too High for St Paul's, frankly, and so I told the bishop."

Gawaine, who knew the bishop moderately well, sympathised with him but did not comment. "He was filling in, I take it – Father Thomas?"

"He was trying to worm his way in," Christabel said crossly, prodding her salmon. "Is that really *fresh*? He'd been abroad somewhere, Africa or India or one of those places – " with a wave of her fork she dismissed the whole of the Third World – "for about ten years, but he'd had to come back because of his health, although personally," she said, sniffing, "I couldn't see that there was anything wrong with him. So the bishop sent him along to St Paul's – and actually let him live in the vicarage – and the next thing we heard, he was letting us all know that he was hoping to stay there permanently!"

To Gawaine, the arrangement sounded exactly what he would have expected from the bishop's practical good sense. "You didn't want him to stay?" he asked.

"Over my dead body!" Christabel snapped, unaware that in the circumstances her comment could have been more happily phrased. "I told the bishop there was no chance of it. And John Bretton – the People's Warden – agreed with me."

12

The unknown Bretton would have had to be a brave man to do anything else. But clearly, with both churchwardens against him, the late Father Thomas would have had no chance at all of being appointed to the living in Ellingwood. Gawaine, who had begun to contemplate the first hint of a motive, dismissed it sorrowfully.

He applied himself to his lunch for a few moments, weighing up the situation. Father Thomas, returning from abroad, with no family close at hand, meaning that Christabel had to be called upon to identify the body, and with scarcely the time or the opportunity to get himself murdered...

"He wasn't liked?" he asked.

"He was not. He'd been in the parish less than three months when he disappeared, and he'd managed to set everyone's backs up."

"That must have taken some dexterity," Gawaine murmured. He called the waitress so Christabel could choose a pudding. "He didn't come at the beginning of your interregnum, then?" he asked when all that was over.

"No, early in July. Absolutely unnecessary – "

As I told the bishop, Gawaine supplied *sotto voce.*

" – we were getting on perfectly well with visiting priests. But the bishop would have it. And of course Father Thomas hadn't been in the place five minutes before everyone was complaining."

"What did he do?" Gawaine asked, in fascinated speculation. What on earth could the wretched man have done to provoke all this hostility? Seduced the Young Wives? Held orgies in the vicarage garden? Celebrated the Black Mass?

"Well, he started to use incense."

Gawaine kept his eyes firmly fixed on the courtyard. The ginger cat was on the move now, pressed to the ground and sneaking up on a sparrow perched on one of the geranium tubs.

Christabel's voice continued. "And of course the sacristan went along with him. All that man ever wants is to find something new for his servers to do. If he likes all that ritual, he should go to Rome and have done with it."

Gawaine gently prompted her away from the iniquities of the sacristan, who was presumably still alive and well, and back to Father Thomas, who was not. The sparrow flew away, and the cat, pretending a total lack of interest in the habits of *passer domesticus domesticus*, sat up and started to wash his ear.

"He hadn't got the least idea of what the congregation needed," Christabel went on. "It wasn't his place to start changing things. Do you know, John Bretton told me, Father Thomas said to him, if he was appointed permanently, he wanted to set up a nave altar. Can you imagine?"

Gawaine shook his head. "Incredible."

"And he started a meditation group on Sundays after Evensong," Christabel continued. "Most undesirable, and not at all appropriate for St Paul's. Not that many people went. I certainly didn't. I've never believed in all this mysticism, and it's never done me any harm."

Gawaine wondered.

"And then," Christabel went on, "there was that awful business about poor Mrs Reed."

Gawaine's interest suddenly sharpened. He could not see anyone being murdered over a dollop of incense or

14

a meditation group, but an injured Mrs Reed might be another matter altogether. "What happened?"

"He refused to give her Communion."

"Oh - why?"

"Because she's been divorced and remarried. And I certainly don't approve of that sort of thing, but her first husband was an absolute pig, as far as one can tell, and she was always so good about the coffee rota and the crèche. And her present husband runs a garden centre, which was very convenient for flowers."

The mention of coffee inspired Gawaine to order it, and he paused until the waitress had served it before he continued.

"What happened - about Mrs Reed?"

"Well, it was referred to the bishop," Christabel said, dumping sugar into her coffee. "I wrote to him myself. But Father Thomas disappeared before there was any decision. You know, so many bishops are reluctant to take a firm line. I don't see what the difficulty is."

Gawaine considered, though naturally he refrained from saying so, that she had just provided him with an excellent argument against the elevation of women to the episcopacy, a development of which he was ordinarily a moderate supporter. Refusing to be sidetracked into a discussion of episcopal rights and duties, he asked, "How did Mrs Reed take it?"

"Well, she was upset... She stopped coming to church, which was very awkward, because I had to do her coffee duty."

"And her husband?" After all, even in these egalitarian times, an offended husband was more likely to be wielding a blunt instrument than a distressed wife.

"I've no idea. Her husband wasn't a member of our congregation. And they aren't the sort of people that I'm in the habit of visiting."

"You must have seen him at his garden centre?"

Christabel froze him with a look, her cat-that-has-been-indiscreet one. "I don't care to discuss church matters with the man in the garden centre."

Gawaine gave up that line of questioning, making a mental note to go and buy a few bulbs as soon as possible. Looking out of the window again, he saw the ginger cat get up, stretch, and go stalking off on feline business of his own. "And who else was upset by Father Thomas?" he asked. "Upset enough to attack him with the traditional blunt instrument, I mean."

"Everybody," Christabel replied darkly, emptying out the last of the coffee from the pot.

"But look, Christabel, no doubt it was all perfectly frightful, I can see that, but after all, you *don't* go and murder a vicar, just because you don't like the way he conducts the service."

Christabel glared at him and gathered herself triumphantly for the last word. "Somebody did," she said.

Chapter Three

...in all our dangers and necessities stretch forth thy right hand to help and defend us.

Collect for the third Sunday after the Epiphany

David Powers spun the wheel and skidded stylishly to a halt in front of Gawaine's house. Switching off the engine, he remained motionless for a few moments. Along with the anxiety and sheer exasperation he felt when his friend insisted on involving himself in another of these affairs, he could not deny a tingle of anticipation. He was stepping out of his usual routine: almost stepping into another world. Apart from the problems which were bound to arise, it would surely be interesting.

There were no lights showing in the house, and when David tugged at the bell pull there was no response. Unfazed, he retrieved the torch from his glove compartment and followed the path that led through the shrubbery and around the side of the house until he was rewarded by seeing a faint oblong of light, filtering onto the ground from the window of the sitting room.

He paused before announcing himself. The room was lit by a log fire, burning low, and a single lamp. Bookshelves and pictures were in shadow. Gawaine, another shadow in a dark blue silk dressing gown, was curled up at one end of the couch. A single streak of light fell on silky golden hair. He was staring out at nothing. He had a note pad in one hand, and there was a scatter of papers on a low table beside him.

David almost felt as if he was looking back through time, into the sanctum of a Victorian gentleman scholar, studying the wisdom of some obscure Greek philosopher, say, or the habits of snails. The illusion persisted, even though David knew that behind the doors of the antique cabinet in one corner there reposed discreetly a television and an up-to-date music system.

He tapped on the window. The stillness broke up as Gawaine, startled, sat up and then crossed the room towards him. "Who's that?"

"Me."

David was aware, for a few seconds, of a look of incredulous relief on Gawaine's face, but naturally, by the time he had trekked back along the path to the now open front door, his friend was all poise and social grace.

"David! How perfectly delightful! Do come in."

David came in and closed the door behind him, following Gawaine as he flitted back towards the sitting room. "Are you out of your tree?" he demanded.

Gawaine halted and turned with a vaguely inquiring expression. "Tree?"

"Batty," David went on. "Nuts. Demented. Is it the full moon or something? Why on earth are you involving yourself – again – in this sort of stuff?"

Gawaine glanced away, then turned back again, looking guilty. "Seff rang you."

"She did, and I don't see why you couldn't ring me yourself." When there was clearly no reply forthcoming

18

– not that David had expected one – he continued, "According to Seff, some female ghoul has press-ganged you. So I brought a weekend bag."

Gawaine's guilty expression dissolved into a reluctant smile. "I'm sure, my dear David, that Persephone didn't mix her metaphors quite so disastrously. Though the substance is perfectly true. My Aunt Christabel – not my actual aunt, as I'm sure you know, my dear David – asked me to take an interest. She's most concerned about the death of her priest."

"We have police for that sort of thing," David pointed out.

"I know." Gawaine said, heading once again to the sitting room. "To be honest, I think she feels there is an aching void in my life which can only be filled by the behests of an aunt."

David suppressed a snort of laughter. "And is there?"

"Who am I to say?" Gawaine responded. "Though at times it's enough to make one feel one is a character in the novels of P G Wodehouse."

"Many murdered vicars in Wodehouse, are there?"

Gawaine shuddered. "Please…"

"You know," David went on, "there's one avenue you haven't explored. You could always say no. N.O. It's easy when you know how."

Gawaine sighed. "I'm afraid I never really learnt it."

And that, David reflected, was the problem. Gawaine was incapable of refusing anyone who asked for his help, from coughing up a few quid for the local cats' home to identifying a murderer. And proving that the unjustly accused were innocent.

Once, that was me.

And for all his airs and graces, David knew that Gawaine's stubborn integrity would never let him give up, no matter what the investigation was costing him. Trying to talk him out of it would always be totally futile.

Following Gawaine into the sitting room, David shrugged out of his coat and dropped into the armchair by the fire. Gawaine's large and dangerous black cat, which was curled up on the rug at his feet, twitched an ear at him and went back to sleep. There was no sign of the little tortoiseshell psychopath; presumably she was out slaying something cute and furry.

"What can I get you?" Gawaine asked, crossing to the drinks table. "Whisky? Brandy? Or do you feel like trying this Armagnac? I'm not really sure about it..."

"Whatever," David said. "And tell me about this dead vicar."

Gawaine handed him a balloon glass with a splash of the dubious Armagnac, and went back to the couch. Curling up again among the cushions he gave David the full story of taking Christabel to identify the vicar's body and hearing her account of how Father Thomas had made himself unpopular in the parish. David listened with interest; there was plenty that didn't add up.

"Doesn't she realise that she's sicking you onto her congregation?" he asked when Gawaine had finished.

"Of course. She's not stupid. Father Thomas had been out of England for more than ten years. It looks almost certain that he was killed because of something that happened in or around St Paul's."

"Unless something from his past had caught up with him," David suggested, stimulated by the problem and the

Armagnac. "Look, he'd been in…Africa, was it? Suppose he stole the eye of the god from some local temple, and he's being hunted down by the fetish priest…"

He was gratified to see that the absurd suggestion had provoked a spark of amusement in Gawaine's expression.

"Really, my dear David, don't you think that a fetish priest in Ellingwood would have been somewhat… noticeable? Mind you, we ought to look into his past. There might be someone with a very old grudge, though if so, the police are better equipped to find him than we are."

"Maybe he was just mugged?"

Gawaine shook his head decidedly. "Oh, no. He was in the vestry, remember, getting ready for the service. Someone must have come along with news so startling that he left the vestry, abandoned his flock to the mercies of the lay reader, and went off without even telling anyone where he was going. He was next seen dead. Whatever made him go out like that must have been pretty powerful."

"And you think it was one of the congregation?"

Gawaine hesitated while he drifted across to replenish the glasses and put another log on the fire, taking care not to disturb the cat.

"Not bad after all, this Armagnac… There's something that doesn't fit," he mused when he was back on the couch. "I said that it's likely he was killed because of something to do with the church, but in that case, who did it? The congregation would be all accounted for, wouldn't they? Patiently waiting for the service to start."

"It would be interesting to see who wasn't."

"It would indeed." Gawaine leant back and gazed dreamily into the fire. David watched him affectionately.

He was pleased that Seff had phoned him, though he wished Gawaine had the confidence to do it himself. He would never have claimed to enjoy these affairs, and he never bothered to hide his disapproval of Gawaine's involving himself, but he still felt the need to be there.

"Your friend Christabel," he said. "Do you suppose..?"

"Not exactly a friend," Gawaine interrupted. "More a kind of…"

He searched for a word and failed to find it. David suspected that he was attempting without success to combine truth with politeness.

"Whoever," David went on. "Her. Do you suppose she knows who wasn't in church that morning? Is she trying to sick you onto someone in particular?"

Gawaine frowned. "I don't know. If it's as simple as that, why not leave it to the police?"

"It just seems odd. I mean, most people want to protect their own little patch, don't they? 'My church, right or wrong.'"

Gawaine's frown deepened. "Oh, I don't think she wants to *protect* anyone."

"But they're her friends, dammit!"

"Not really," Gawaine responded. "Or at least, only so long as they behave themselves. If one of her friends so far forgot himself as to commit murder, he would find himself out in the cold pretty quickly."

"She sounds charming. Are you sure she didn't swipe this bloke herself?"

Gawaine's frown cleared and he gave David an intent look as if he had just said something rather clever. David couldn't imagine what.

"By no means," Gawaine said. "Even though she called me in. She would assess my intelligence as roughly equivalent to that of a goldfish." He considered his simile. "A retarded goldfish."

A companiable silence fell. Gawaine looked drowsy, and far more relaxed than he had done when David arrived. The room was peaceful. David, sipping Armagnac, found it progressively more difficult to apply his mind to the topic of violent death.

"What are you going to do?" he asked with an effort.

Gawaine came to himself, the languid blue eyes suddenly wide and alert. "Do? Oh, Christabel has it all well in hand. It's obvious there are three areas of inquiry - Father Thomas's past in this country, his past in Africa, and his present involvement with St Paul's. There's not a lot I can do about the first two, but I can look into the third. So I'm invited to church on Sunday morning, followed by pre-lunch drinks, followed by lunch, so that I can meet the congregation, or at least that portion of it Christabel wishes me to meet."

"Are those suspects, or people she thinks are her social equals?"

"That's a good question, my dear David. Both, I should say. Of course, it will all be perfectly frightful. I don't suppose that you..." He was starting to look distressed again.

"I told you," David replied, "I'm here for the weekend. I'll come, if she'll have me. Mind you, I'm damned if I'm coming to church."

Forbearing to comment on a certain lack of logic in this final remark, Gawaine got up and drifted out into the hall to the telephone. He returned in a few minutes, looking satisfied.

"You are invited," he announced, "provided, and I quote, that you are not 'that floozie you picked up in the car park'. The floozie being Persephone. I was able to reassure her."

He did not return to the sofa, but sat on a pouffe at David's feet and poked the fire meditatively. The cat woke and turned his head to give him a filthy look, then stalked off through the half-open door on affairs of his own.

"So we can't do any more till Sunday?" David asked.

"Indeed we can." Gawaine tried and failed to look affronted. "*I* am running this investigation, not Christabel. And there are other openings. I rang the bishop earlier," he went on, "but I only got his secretary. I left a message. I felt it wasn't quite the done thing to go poking around in his diocese without letting him know – and if he doesn't object to me on principle, he might be able to tell me quite a lot about Father Thomas."

"That would help."

Gawaine nodded. "I never met him, and how can I find out who killed him if I don't know what sort of a man he was? I don't pay any attention to what Christabel said, of course. What I really need is to find someone who liked him."

"There must have been someone," said David.

Gawaine shrugged. "Not if you listen to Christabel. And another thing," he added. "Tomorrow we are going to buy some bulbs."

"Bulbs?"

"Daffodils. Jonquils. Fritillaries, maybe. From the garden centre run by Mrs Reed's husband."

"Oh – right. But you don't expect that she liked Father Thomas, when he kicked her out?"

Gawaine flashed him a look, then went back to contemplating the fire. "He did not precisely 'kick her out'. I need to get her version of that story. It seems a poor motive for murder, but one never knows. By the way, have you eaten?"

Surprised by the change of subject, David replied that no, he had not eaten. He did not exactly want to admit that immediately after Seff's phone call he had stuffed everything in sight into a bag and scorched his way out of London at such speed that he had been extremely lucky not to pick up a handful of tickets.

"I'm terribly sorry," Gawaine said, "but Mrs Summers has gone. Still, you could scramble some eggs, couldn't you…if we have eggs?"

"Any idiot can scramble eggs."

David was fairly sure, even so, that Gawaine probably didn't belong in the category of 'any idiot'.

"Then feel free, my dear David," Gawaine said composedly. "And I shall make some coffee. And we shall do our best to shelve the problem of Father Thomas until tomorrow."

Chapter Four

If any of you know cause, or just impediment, why
these two persons should not be joined together in Holy
Matrimony, ye are to declare it.

The Form of Solemnisation of Matrimony.

On the following morning, Gawaine was once again
dragged out of bed at what he considered an unearthly
hour by a telephone call from the bishop. David, at
breakfast in the dining room, heard Gawaine's half of a long
conversation coming from the hall, although frustratingly
he was unable to catch more than a word or two. He called
out as he heard the phone being put down, and Gawaine
appeared in the doorway, looking ruffled and drowsy.

"What was all that about?" David asked.

Gawaine gestured vaguely. "The bishop."

"I gathered it was the bishop. I want to know what he
said."

There was a few seconds when he thought Gawaine
might actually go back to sleep where he stood.

"Come and have some breakfast," he suggested.

Gawaine shuddered. "At this time?"

"Most people seem to think it's a fairly good time."

Gawaine's shudder intensified, but he condescended
to come into the room and sit down opposite David.

Mrs Summers, his housekeeper, appeared promptly on cue with an extra cup and a fresh pot of coffee. She set both of these in front of Gawaine with the housekeeperly equivalent of a dirty look, and withdrew.

"You don't deserve that woman," David remarked.

"Too true."

Gawaine concentrated grimly on aiming coffee at his cup. David continued with his own meal, which was excellent. He suspected that Mrs Summers had a secret passion for breakfast, and that she would have been supremely happy filling the row of silver chafing dishes which are supposed to adorn an English gentleman's sideboard, a satisfaction she was never to enjoy, since Gawaine regularly started the day with nothing more substantial than black coffee.

"How can anyone," Gawaine said plaintively, "expect an intelligent response at this time in the morning?"

David was not sure whether Gawaine meant him or the bishop, and did not ask. He allowed his friend a few moments alone with the coffee, before he reminded him, "The phone call?"

"Oh, yes – that."

Had he been this vague with the bishop, David wondered, or was it all an elaborate act? Or had an episcopal phone call taken so much out of him that he was fit for nothing but a quick return to bed?

"He got my message." Gawaine paused, seemed to realise this piece of information was superfluous, and went on, sounding mildly surprised. "He seemed quite pleased. He thought it would be a good idea to have someone to keep an eye on the Church's interest." He paused again and refilled his coffee cup. "At any rate, he's going to send me some information on Father Thomas's background, and make it known that I have his authority in case anyone questions what I'm doing."

"Useful," David commented.

"Very. If that congregation are anything like Christabel, they're going to start questioning like mad. And he's going to have a word with the police officer in charge of the case. In fact, he's doing everything he can to smooth my path."

He sighed deeply and fell silent, looking rather discouraged.

"Actually," David said, "you would rather he told you to mind your own business." *Not that it would make any difference if he did*, he added to himself.

Gawaine nodded, forcing a faint smile. "On pain of excommunication. True. But as it is... Oh well, my dear David, at least it gives me the opportunity of indulging in my worst vice."

Which, as he had often said – preventing David from the contemplation of nameless evils – was curiosity.

About an hour later, when David had finished his breakfast and Gawaine, showered and dressed, was restored to something resembling a functional human being, they made a start for Ellingwood.

David was driving. He had looked up Reed's Garden Centre on the internet, and found it was located on the edge of the village, about as far away from Christabel's house as it could possibly be. This suited Gawaine. He had planned a swift raid, in and out, without Christabel's knowing he had been in the vicinity.

"Or she would certainly," he commented, "find something to complain about."

"I'm assuming," David began as he drove out of Gawaine's drive rather more circumspectly than he had driven in, "that it's a big deal, if your vicar refuses to give you Communion."

Gawaine murmured agreement.

"But if it bothered you enough to want to murder him…" David pursued his line of thought while negotiating a roundabout ahead of a Volkswagen Beetle with delusions of grandeur. "…then you must be…well, religious enough not to actually do it. 'Thou shalt not kill', and all that."

"Indeed." Gawaine sighed. "But people do strange things."

David was not afflicted with any of Gawaine's problems in navigation, and found the Garden Centre without even needing to use his satnav. It was large, and looked prosperous. There were several cars in the car park, and groups of people wandering up and down the rows of plants. Children played on swings and a slide. Further away to the right were two or three large greenhouses, and on the left was a kind of patio arrangement displaying garden furniture, which led to a long wooden building with a sign reading 'SALES'.

"So how do you propose to get Mrs Reed to tell you what happened between her and Father Thomas?" David asked as he drew into a parking space.

Gawaine flashed him a glance. "I know it's a radical concept, my dear David, but I imagined that I would ask her."

David had his doubts about that. Asking personal questions was likely to result in a flea in the ear, if not a call to the local cops. "There's hardly been time for the bishop to pass the word," he pointed out.

"True," Gawaine said. "We shall just have to go in on a wing and – quite appropriately – a prayer."

They got out of the car and made their way towards the building, passing a display of garishly coloured lawn ornaments.

"One day," David remarked, "I'm going to give you a fishing gnome for your lily pond."

Gawaine essayed, not very successfully, a look of freezing contempt, and did not deign to reply. David guessed that for all his insouciance he was growing worried about the coming interview. After all, how did you approach a complete stranger and demand to know the intimate details of her personal life? Actually, he thought, if you were Gawaine, you did it with exquisite courtesy and a disarming lack of pretension – a devastating technique that was all the more effective because he was entirely unconscious of it.

Inside the building were the usual displays of seeds and garden tools, and a row of brightly coloured plastic bins filled with different kinds of bulbs. Gawaine drifted over to these, and with rather more animation than he had shown all day, began to fill a bag.

"What do you think you're doing?" David asked.

Gawaine smiled at him amiably. "Buying bulbs. That bit of shrubbery near the front gate is terribly boring until the rhododendrons come out."

David had never shared the English passion for a garden. As far as he was concerned, Repton was a computer game. But he knew that Gawaine, while appearing far too elegant and impractical ever to set hand to trowel, managed his garden far more efficiently than he managed the rest of his life. He was buying bulbs, not as a cover, or to ingratiate himself with the Reeds, but because he was genuinely interested, and would just as soon forget his real reason for coming.

While Gawaine made his choice, David took a closer look around him. There was a cash desk with a grey-haired woman on duty, and he wondered if this might be Mrs Reed. He had imagined someone younger, but no one had actually mentioned her age.

Further down the building, a younger woman was restocking shelves. She had her back to David, and all he could see was that she was tall, with long fair hair down her back in a single braid. Her figure was good enough to interest him, and when she turned and came up to the cash desk, he was impressed with the front view of her, too. Then she spoke to the woman on the till, and he heard her reply.

"That's right, Mrs Reed."

David touched Gawaine's arm, disturbing him in the rapt contemplation of the rival merits of fritillaries and scillas, and nodded towards their quarry, who had gone back to her shelves.

"That's her."

Gawaine smiled at him abstractedly. "Who?"

"Mrs Reed, for goodness' sake!" David returned in a savage whisper.

"Really?" Gawaine sighed. "All right, my dear David, just let me pay for this lot."

David could not see the projected conversation taking place at all comfortably over a sack of bulbs, and offered to take it out to the car. When he returned, Gawaine was at the far end of the building, already talking to Mrs Reed, who was listening with a wary look. David approached and was introduced.

"I'm terribly sorry," Gawaine went on, picking up the thread of what he had been saying. 'I know the last thing you'll want is to talk about your personal affairs to a pair of complete strangers."

"I've nothing to hide," Mrs Reed said automatically and without hostility. "If I can help…"

"It would help a great deal," Gawaine assured her, "if you would tell us what happened between you and Father Thomas."

"Poor man. We just heard about him. What a shocking thing."

Her regret seemed genuine, but David wondered if she was really sorry. Father Thomas had not treated her well, but had he treated her badly enough for her to have a serious grievance?

"All right," she decided. "You'd better come over to the house."

She led the way out of the building and down a path towards a white bungalow beyond the greenhouses. About half way there they were met by a man coming the other way – a big man, tall and burly, in workman's overalls. He stopped on the path a yard or two away and loomed over them. "Any trouble, Ruth?" he asked.

"No, it's okay, Frank," Mrs Reed replied. "It's about Father Thomas."

"Oh?" The man – evidently Mr Reed – loomed for a short while longer. Then he gave a curt nod. "Call me if you want me," he said, and went on.

When they reached the bungalow, Mrs Reed took them round the back and into the kitchen. A girl of about eight, thin and dark, sat painting at the kitchen table. A much smaller boy was bouncing up and down in a playpen, gurgling cheerfully. "Claire," Mrs Reed said, "take Robin down to the swing for half an hour."

"I want to finish my painting, Mummy. I'll take him in a minute."

"*Now*, Claire."

"Okay."

The girl put down her brush, with a grin to show her mother there were no hard feelings, hauled the little boy out of the playpen and disappeared with him through the door. David thought Mrs Reed relaxed slightly when they were gone.

"Sit down," she invited them. "I hope you don't mind the kitchen, but I ought to start lunch. You'll have some coffee?"

She was putting the kettle on as she spoke. Gawaine and David found themselves seats; Gawaine studied the abandoned painting with some care.

"I believe Father Thomas refused you Communion?" he asked diffidently.

"That's right."

"I'm sorry, it's frightfully impertinent, but how did you feel about that?"

Mrs Reed swung round from the work surface, the coffee jar in her hand. David wondered if she was going to answer. He suspected that she was wondering as well.

Eventually she said, "I suppose if I'm going to talk to you at all, I'd better tell you everything. If it'll help you find out who did that dreadful thing to Father Thomas – "

"You're sorry he's dead?" David interposed.

Her voice sharpened. "Of course I'm sorry he's dead! What do you take me for?"

David murmured an apology and resolved to stay quiet. Gawaine managed these things much better on his own.

"I was upset." Mrs Reed answered the original question. "But I could understand it. He was only doing what he thought was right."

"It hadn't been a problem before?" Gawaine inquired.

"No. The vicar – the old vicar who left, Jim Trask – he knew all about it. You see…"

She paused as she poured boiling water into the coffee mugs and brought them to the table with milk and sugar.

"I came here three years ago," she explained. "When I married Frank. I already had Claire so I couldn't hide that I'd been married before. I suppose I could have said I was a widow, but I'm not ashamed of what I did, and anyway these days most people couldn't care less. Besides, when you start telling lies like that you never stop, and somebody always finds out in the end. I wanted to go to church, and I talked to Jim, and it was all right. There were reasons…"

She drank some of her own coffee. Gawaine remained silent, looking encouraging.

"I was far too young when I got married at first," Mrs Reed went on. "Steve – that was my first husband – drank a lot, and he used to hit me. I left him once, but I went back. Then after I had Claire, he started to hit her when she cried, so then I knew I had to get out. I got a divorce all right – I could have got a divorce three times over. Then after a bit I met Frank and married him. There was never any problem until Father Thomas came."

She stopped, drained her coffee mug and took it over to the sink. "You won't mind if I get on with these carrots?" Whether they minded or not, she started scraping.

"And then?" Gawaine asked delicately.

"Well. Father Thomas said I couldn't come to Communion unless I repented and amended my life." She shook her head, looking more exasperated than upset. "Well, I ask you! That would have meant leaving Frank, and what would have happened to the children? But I couldn't make him see it."

"So what did you do?"

Mrs Reed shrugged. "Stopped going to church at all for a bit. I had to think things out. I believe Mrs Cottesmore wrote to the bishop about it, but honestly, she could have saved herself the trouble. Then after a couple of weeks or so I had a phone call from the vicar of St John's – that's the next parish. He said would I come and have a talk to him. So – well, the upshot of it all is that I go to St John's now, and to tell you the truth…" She hesitated and then went on. "I feel I fit in there a lot better than I did at St Paul's. They're a bit of a clique, you know."

Gawaine nodded. "You didn't get on with…say with Mrs Cottesmore?"

"Oh, I got on with her all right, just so long as I knew my place. She called me Ruth, but she'd have had a fit if I'd called her Christabel."

She relaxed a little, with the first gleam of humour she had shown through all the conversation. "So are you going to ask me where I was at nine o'clock that Sunday morning?"

Gawaine looked genuinely shocked. "I shouldn't dream of it," he protested.

"Because I don't mind," Mrs Reed said. "I was on my way to church. St John's. With the children."

There seemed no need to disbelieve her, and nothing more to be said. Gawaine took his leave gracefully.

Mrs Reed escorted them out onto the path, and said in farewell, "I hope you find him, whoever he was. You know, I wasn't angry with Father Thomas. He was a good man. He just hadn't any..." She searched for a word. "... any common sense."

And that, David thought, as they retraced their steps to the garden centre and the car, could have been a comment on Gawaine himself.

"Well?" he asked as he manoeuvred out onto the road.

"If that woman committed a murder, you may buy me that fishing gnome."

"She knew a fair bit about it, though."

"My dear David!" Gawaine turned wide blue eyes on him. "A small village. The only thing in the universe faster than light is gossip. No, that isn't what's on my mind."

David concentrated on his driving, and refrained from asking what was. It would appear soon enough.

After a few minutes' thought, Gawaine went on, "If she has an alibi, what about her husband? He wasn't with her. Not a churchgoer, according to Christabel."

David trod on the brake and fumed behind an ambling tractor. "You're not telling me he did in the vicar because he insulted his wife? Come on!"

36

"Stop cursing that tractor, my dear David. It's bad for your blood pressure. No – you haven't grasped the situation. Father Thomas was threatening his marriage. Suppose Mrs Reed had taken him seriously? Suppose she had left her husband? He would have lost his wife and his son."

"She wouldn't…"

"No, but did he think she would?"

Resigning himself to crawling along in the tractor's wake, David thought it over. "Perhaps he went to talk it over with Father Thomas?" he suggested. "He's a big chap. Maybe he lost his temper and hit him a bit harder than he meant to."

Gawaine shuddered slightly. "Not impossible," he conceded. "But he'd hardly go and talk to him just before the service. I hate to say this, but if Frank Reed did it, he meant to do it."

He winced and closed his eyes as David spotted an opening and roared through it. "I'd really like to know," he said faintly, "just where Frank Reed was at nine o'clock that morning."

Chapter Five

...they have heard with their ears only, and their heart, spirit and mind, have not been edified thereby.

Concerning the Service of the Church

St Paul's was a medieval church, but the glass was indifferent Victorian. Gawaine had plenty of opportunity to study it before that Sunday morning's service started. Organised as far as the church by David, for what he considered to be the appallingly uncivilised hour of nine fifteen – his own parish church began operations at a more moderate ten thirty – and organised into a pew by Christabel, he was by now resigned to what the day might bring.

There were compensations, notably an organist who was better than competent, and a choir who were trying their best to do him justice. The service was middle-of-the-road Anglican rather than Anglo-Catholic, the direction in which Father Thomas had been trying to move it, with candles and a procession, but definitely no incense.

He could not help being distracted from spiritual matters by trying to identify the characters in the story of the murder of Father Thomas. Most of them were presumably in church; it was quite likely that the murderer was in church. The presiding clergyman, of course, had nothing to do with the matter; he was another visitor.

Leading the intercessions was a tall, fair man whose blue scarf identified him as the lay reader who had taken the service when Father Thomas had disappeared. Gawaine also thought he could identify the sacristan, who was youngish, plump, with receding brown hair and a distinctly mischievous look.

At the point in the service when the Epistle was read, Christabel gave Gawaine a savage jab in the ribs and whispered, "John Bretton." He assumed she was naming the reader. He was a short man, stocky, middle-aged but still dark-haired, vigorous-looking, with a resonant delivery. The other churchwarden, and by the look of him no yes-man for Christabel. Gawaine wondered whether he had an alibi for that Sunday morning.

A shiver ran through Gawaine as the congregation began to line up to go to the altar rail and take Communion. Could you murder your vicar and still receive the sacrament? That would be evidence of some seriously messed-up thinking, but then, Gawaine reflected, your thinking would have to be pretty messed up to commit the murder in the first place. He tried to see if anyone was staying put in the pew, but in the midst of the constant coming and going, and the added confusion when the Junior Church arrived, he couldn't be sure.

At the end of the service, Gawaine would have been quite happy to linger and listen to the organist playing Bach, but Christabel hustled him purposefully out of church. Gawaine was startled, during this hasty departure, to see Seff seated demurely in a pew at the back. She gave him a flashing smile, but Christabel, with an audible snort, allowed him no opportunity to speak.

"Really!" she exclaimed when they were heading down the path to the lychgate. "How that woman has the face! No better than she should be, mark my words."

Gawaine would have thought, though naturally he did not say so, that attendance at church might be interpreted as a sign of grace. He allowed Christabel to pilot him across the road to the car park and into the church hall, where coffee was being served. He noticed as he did so that David's red sports car was parked conspicuously near the hall door, but David was not with it. He had given David a job before they separated: to walk around the village and to make a sketch map of possible approaches to the church, in the hope of discovering the route which the murderer had used. Presumably David was still at it, or perhaps, Gawaine thought wistfully, he had retired to the village pub.

The church hall was like all church halls, large and bare with a curtained stage at one end. Coffee was being served from trestle tables below the stage. There was a bookstall and someone selling home made jam.

Christabel abandoned Gawaine in the middle of the hall and ploughed her way into the coffee queue. He waited, feeling somewhat surplus to requirements, then jumped as someone said into his right ear, "Hello. Are you new? Would you like some coffee?"

Gawaine turned. It was a woman who had spoken: about forty, plump and slightly scatty-looking, giving him a friendly smile. He introduced himself.

"Oh lord, you're Christabel's sleuth!"

Gawaine winced, and the woman clapped a hand over her mouth.

40

"Sorry! I shouldn't have said that, should I? I'm always putting my foot in it."

Her distress was comical, and in spite of himself Gawaine found that he was returning her smile. "I hope Christabel isn't spreading the word all round the parish," he murmured.

"If she hasn't, she will." The woman thought about that remark and added, "Was that catty?"

"Very. Also, unfortunately, true."

"I ought to be more careful what I say. My husband tells me all the time." She gave Gawaine a conspiratorial giggle. "It was when I was in church yesterday. I was dusting, and Christabel was doing the flowers. I overheard her telling George – that's the sacristan – all about you." Defensively, she concluded, "I couldn't help overhearing."

Gawaine accepted that given Christabel's normal style of delivery, it would be impossible for anyone in the same church not to overhear.

"Actually, I listened," the woman confided with another giggle. "It was interesting. And I hope you do find out who killed Father Thomas."

"You liked him?" Gawaine inquired, feeling obliged to do a little detecting.

"Yes, I did." There was a defiant note in her voice, as if she felt she was going out on a rather precarious limb. "Most people didn't, because he wasn't a bit like Jim Trask, and he wanted to change things. But I didn't see that it mattered all that much. I mean, what's the point of getting worked up over a bit of incense, or where you put the altar? It's not important, is it?"

"Did you know Father Thomas well?"

"Oh, no, not *well*. Not many people did. He wasn't here long enough. But I suppose I did know him a bit better than most people here. I went to his meditation group, for one thing."

Oh yes, Gawaine remembered. *Nameless orgies in the vicarage after Evensong.*

"What was it like?" he asked.

"Oh, really helpful!" There was no mistaking her enthusiasm; Gawaine felt his interest quickening. "Have you ever tried it – Ignatian meditation? I've always found prayer really hard, but this was different." She hesitated, deliberately checking herself. "My husband didn't really like me going. And he wouldn't come himself, to see what it was like. Oh, well…" She shrugged. "It was only for a few weeks, because then Father Thomas disappeared. I do hope – "

She broke off as Christabel bore down on them, bearing coffee.

"Thank you, Jennifer." Christabel's voice was arctic. "How kind of you to look after Gawaine. Do you know your little boy is playing with the curtains?"

"Oh, goodness!" Flustered, Jennifer took a step or two toward the stage, where the curtains were jerkily opening. Then she looked back at Gawaine. "I do hope everything goes well," she said, and hurried off.

Warmth and cheerfulness went with her. Gawaine thanked Christabel for his coffee, realised that she had put both milk and sugar in it, and looked around for somewhere he could get rid of it discreetly.

"A remarkably silly woman," Christabel pronounced. "And always pushing herself forward. I hope you don't think she would have anything useful to tell you."

Gawaine might, if he had dared, have told her that he would be the best judge of that. Someone sympathetic to Father Thomas could be very useful to him, and he wondered how he might get in touch with her again. She was obviously not destined to be among those present at Christabel's lunch party. And there was a husband who sounded as if he might be a problem. Temporarily Gawaine put Jennifer and the possible help she could give him on what he had heard David describe as the back burner.

Before Christabel could offer any more charitable remarks, they were joined by Charles Cottesmore, her husband. He was a quiet, self-sufficient man, as indeed he would have to be to survive marriage to Christabel. Gawaine did not know him well, but liked what he knew.

"Where have you been?" Christabel snapped.

"Counting the collection," her husband returned, unruffled.

"I need to get away. We do have sixteen people coming for lunch."

Charles Cottesmore smiled equably. "Mrs Wilson will have it all in hand," he reassured her, thereby blighting any impression Christabel might have been trying to cultivate that she and she only was responsible for the lunch.

"I hope you put the wine in the fridge," she retorted, going into the attack again.

"Of course."

"Then let's be on our way. Drink your coffee, Gawaine."

Gawaine looked helplessly at the murky brew in his cup. He was rescued by Charles Cottesmore, who took it away from him and deposited it on a passing tray.

Muttering impatiently, Christabel rounded them both up and began shepherding them towards the door. However, before they reached it, they were intercepted by the young man Gawaine had identified – correctly, as it turned out – as the sacristan. He seized Gawaine's hand and shook it enthusiastically.

"This the chap you were telling me about?" he asked Christabel, impervious to the look she was giving him, which was potentially as lethal as a scythe on a chariot wheel. "Very glad to meet you. I'm George Marshall – sacristan. Look, I've got to dash, but if you want to come over to the church a bit later on – say five o'clock – I can fill you in."

"I've already told him what he needs to know," Christabel snapped.

The sacristan smiled at her with unabated good humour. "Oh, yes, but he'll want to see where it all happened, won't he? See you," he added to Gawaine. "Five o'clockish. Okay?"

Gawaine murmured an assent as George veered off towards the coffee.

"Really!" Christabel exclaimed.

She led the way rapidly out to the car park before anyone else got a chance to hold them up. This time, to Gawaine's relief, David was there, sitting in his car, and Gawaine was able to introduce him. He was looking wary; in view of what was to come, Gawaine could not help feeling that he had good reason.

Chapter Six

Defend us thy humble servants in all assaults of our enemies.

The Collect for Peace

Christabel's drawing room was large, and would have been pleasant, if Gawaine had not felt that everything in it had been put in its place and firmly told to stay there. Including the guests. He sipped a glass of dry sherry, thankful that it was Charles Cottesmore and not Christabel who was responsible for the wine. Looking around for David, he saw that his friend had been snaffled by a man and – presumably – his wife, who were unknown to him, and was hemmed in close by the patio doors. Seconds later, someone came and planted himself in front of Gawaine, stuck out a hand and said, "Bretton. Churchwarden."

Gawaine identified him as the short, vigorous man who had read the lesson in church. He was not looking friendly, and as Gawaine shook the proffered hand he added uncompromisingly, "Christabel told me about you. Lot of damned nonsense, if you ask me."

There was not much that anyone could say in reply to that, but Bretton seemed not to need a reply, and steamed on regardless of what Gawaine's reaction might be.

45

"Last thing we want is publicity. That bloody reporter was sniffing around here again this morning. Christabel says you know her?"

"Yes, she…" Gawaine murmured, but Bretton was not really listening. You might have needed a pneumatic drill to insert a word edgeways into this conversation.

"Not the sort of thing we want to encourage," Bretton went on. "Bad for the Church."

Bad for Father Thomas, too. Gawaine sighed faintly and sipped more sherry. He was well aware that his appearance would not impress Bretton, who probably liked his detectives hard-boiled, with gats.

"What d'you intend doing?" With that question, fired like a bullet from the aforementioned gat, Bretton came to an abrupt halt.

"Oh…" Gawaine responded. "Meet people, wander around…ask a few questions."

Bretton's snort gave his opinion of that programme.

"For example, were you in church that morning, Mr Bretton? The day that Father Thomas disappeared?"

Bretton gave him a scorching look. "For what good it will do you, no, I wasn't. I had work to do."

"Work?"

Gawaine left the word poised delicately in the air. For a minute he thought he might have lost Bretton altogether, and then the churchwarden replied, "I'm Head of Ellingwood Court."

He spoke as if that institution should have been well-known enough to need no explanation. Gawaine struggled briefly with memory – Borstal, loony bin? – until he identified it, with relief, as a boys' prep school, and one with a good reputation in the area. Bretton was a surprising Head; Gawaine had thought they were an altogether gentler breed these days. He would certainly have no problems disciplining the boys, although perhaps the parents gave more trouble, or perhaps he had a different tone of voice for parents or prospective parents.

Gawaine dragged his mind away from the contemplation of educational fashion to take notice of what Bretton was saying.

"I spent the day preparing for a Governors' meeting. We're planning a new building, and I had to go over the accounts."

"Alone?"

If Bretton had been a bull – which, a little, he resembled – he would have been snorting and pawing the ground. But he answered. "Yes, alone. I had lunch with my wife and daughter, and finished about mid afternoon. Came to Evensong."

It occurred to Gawaine that Bretton was answering because of the power of Christabel's personality. It certainly was not because of his own personality, or Bretton's urge for investigation. Perhaps there was something to be said for Christabel after all.

"What do you think happened to Father Thomas?" he ventured.

Bretton shrugged. "Mugged, probably."

"But that doesn't explain why he left the vestry just before the service."

Though Bretton was standing a yard or so away, and made no move towards him, Gawaine had the sensation of being grabbed by a handful of shirt front.

"Look, I don't have to explain it. I wouldn't try explaining anything that chap did, or didn't do. He wasn't right in the head."

Gawaine was startled. So far no one had tried to explain Father Thomas's behaviour in terms of actual madness. "Literally?" he asked.

"How should I know? But the way he carried on... Let me give you a case in point."

He seemed to be calming down. Obviously he preferred discussing Father Thomas when alive to accounting for his own movements on the day of his death.

"There's always been a tradition that the Vicar of St Paul's acts as Chaplain to Ellingwood Court. Nothing much to it – turn up at the final assembly of term, and talk to the boys once or twice a year. Well, with Trask, who was here before – no problem. But Father Thomas – my God, he was dynamite!"

"Really?"

"He came here towards the end of the summer term, so there wasn't much chance to get his measure. But then he came and took an assembly. He spoke about the rich young ruler – sell all you have and give to the poor, you know?"

Gawaine indicated a familiarity with that particular portion of Holy Scripture.

"Spoke well, I'll give him that. But the next thing I know, I've got a parent on the phone. This lad had gone and given his personal computer – a thousand quid's worth of stuff – to the local Oxfam shop. Father was furious. I went down there, and thank God I managed to buy it back. And there were two or three others – not so dramatic. Parents didn't like it. One threatened to take his son away if there was a repetition. And if you're thinking – " he leant forward and gave Gawaine a prod – "if you're thinking I killed Father Thomas so there wouldn't be a repetition, you can think again. I just told him that was the last time I'd invite him."

"And how did he feel about that?" Gawaine inquired.

"He didn't like it, but there wasn't much he could do about it. Besides, he wouldn't have been here much longer. There was never the remotest chance that we would give him the living."

Gawaine thought that over. He could have done with a breathing-space. Bretton had presented him with a viable motive. Parents threatening to take their sons away must be a headmaster's most frequent nightmare. Gawaine did not necessarily believe that Bretton had been satisfied to warn Father Thomas off. He was certainly capable of violence, and he had not been in church on the morning Father Thomas disappeared, though it would be rash to assume he had no alibi. Had anyone seen him working on his accounts? Had his wife, for example, taken him coffee? There was a lot to think about and follow up, but Gawaine could not believe that Bretton would take kindly to having his nearest and dearest questioned.

Bretton gave Gawaine a curt nod, and moved away. Gawaine looked among the crowd for David, but before he managed to spot him, he felt a hand clamping itself on his shoulder, and glanced around to see a stocky, elderly man with white hair in a military cut, and a bristling moustache. His face was lined and reddened; he looked like someone who would have been found defending the borders of Empire, if the Empire had still existed.

"You're this chap of Christabel's," he informed Gawaine.

Gawaine murmured agreement.

"Colonel Sutton," the man introduced himself, releasing Gawaine's shoulder to seize his hand in a bone-pulverising grip. "Terrible business. Glad to see that someone is taking it seriously."

"I'll do my best," Gawaine responded, surreptitiously flexing his fingers and wondering whether he would ever play the piano again.

"Stout fellow!" The colonel took a gulp of wine, and repeated, "Terrible business, this. Great loss."

Startled that anyone still talked like that, Gawaine took a moment to process what he had actually said. "You *liked* Father Thomas?"

"Oh, yes. Splendid chap. None of your wishy-washy liberal ideas. Not afraid to stand up for good old-fashioned moral values."

Gawaine wondered what Colonel Sutton meant by that. The colonel struck him as the kind of man who might well regret the passing of the birch and transportation.

"Really?" he murmured. "How interesting. So the… difficulty with Ruth Reed – ?"

"Father Thomas was absolutely right," the Colonel said. "And I don't care who hears me say it. We don't want people like that in the church! What sort of an example does it set?"

"Then you would have supported Father Thomas's application for the living?"

"I certainly would. If we'd had Father Thomas with us a couple of years ago, there never would have been all that fuss about that wretched woman Chantal."

"Chantal?" Gawaine queried, feeling the first flicker of interest.

The colonel waved him away. "Nothing for you to worry about," he said. "That was back in Jim Trask's time, long before Father Thomas set foot in the parish." He swigged the last of his wine. "Good luck to you," he added, and pottered off to look for a refill.

Before Gawaine could give any thought to what he had learnt, Christabel began to round up her guests for lunch, with all the determination though none of the style of a sheepdog at trials. Gawaine found himself herded into the dining room, where a buffet style meal was laid out. He filled a plate, accepted the glass of wine that Charles Cottesmore handed to him, and began looking round rather desperately by now for David, since he felt in urgent need of being rescued.

David, however, had totally vanished, and since Christabel's guests were dispersing themselves widely over the house and garden, looking for congenial spots in which to sit and eat, Gawaine felt that he might make himself conspicuous by going to look for him.

He stepped out of the dining room, which also boasted patio doors, onto the promised patio, which was adorned by white-painted chairs and tables, and stripy umbrellas, strongly reminiscent of the Costa del Whatever, and by an assortment of singularly uninteresting shrubs, in pots. Gawaine looked around uncertainly. No one was paying him much attention. Still no David.

Close by the patio wall a woman was sitting by herself, sipping a glass of wine. She looked rather out of place among Christabel's guests. She was small and thin, her mousy hair frizzed up in a tight perm. Her frock would never have found favour with Christabel, who dressed at Harrods and beyond.

Gawaine drifted over. "Do you mind if I join you?"

"Oh no, please do." She gazed at him nervously as he took a vacant chair. "You're Christabel's friend, aren't you?"

Gawaine admitted it.

"She says you're awfully clever."

Mentally promising himself to speak to Christabel later – a promise he knew would never be fulfilled – Gawaine told her his name and consciously tried not to look awfully clever.

"I'm Louise Braid," his companion said. "Wasn't it dreadful about Father Thomas?"

This question brought Gawaine onto safer ground. He agreed that it was indeed dreadful, and asked Louise if she had been in church on the morning in question.

"Oh, yes," Louise replied. "At least, I was in the hall, getting the coffee ready. It was my week for the coffee rota. So by the time I actually got into church, everyone was already looking for Father Thomas, and a few minutes later Malcolm started the service."

"Malcolm?"

Louise simpered a bit, with pride. "My brother. He's the lay reader."

She half pointed down to the other end of the patio. There was a large group of people, including Christabel herself, and the tall, fair, very handsome man who had worn the blue scarf during the service. He seemed to be on the point of leaving them, but had too much to say to them all actually to do so. Gawaine thought that if he had to socialise so heartily he might have done it without leaving his sister by herself.

"He's a solicitor," Louise said, "so he has to keep in with everybody."

The apparently artless remark startled Gawaine. Was she as innocent as she seemed, trying to excuse her brother for being thoughtless, or had there been an undertone of malice? He took another look at Louise.

"Isn't this paté delicious?" she asked with a girlish little giggle. "Christabel doesn't make it herself, you know."

Definitely malice. Gawaine could not help wondering if Louise was by herself because everyone who knew her got tired of being needled, and also could not help asking himself if she had really been preparing coffee on that particular morning. Coffee duty in the hall would be an excellent excuse for not being in church at the time Father Thomas disappeared.

"Father Thomas didn't come into the hall that morning?" he asked, hoping that his innocent demeanour equalled Louise's own.

"Oh, no. At least, I didn't see him." She brought his suspicions crashing about his ears by adding, "You could ask Jennifer Rook. She was on duty with me. She's not here now, of course. She's not really our sort of person."

That must be the Jennifer who had spoken to him in the church hall. Gawaine promised himself another word with her. He did not think it likely that Father Thomas had gone anywhere near the hall, but he would like to be sure that the catty Louise had been where she said she had. The trouble was, he knew, that she would not have suggested he talked to Jennifer if Jennifer could have said anything remotely harmful. Besides, he had no reason so far for suspecting Louise Braid of wanting to remove her parish priest, and she looked too small and slender to have murdered him and then disposed of his body.

Unless she had help...

At this point in his musings the tall fair man finally made his farewells to the other group and came over to his sister. Light blue eyes, rather too prominent, bored into Gawaine.

"Oh, Malcolm," Louise said with a fetching little trill, "this is Christabel's friend, Gawaine St Clair. He's going to find out everything we've got to hide!"

Chapter Seven

Cursed is he that removeth his neighbour's landmark.

A Commination

David had expected to feel out of place spending Sunday among Christabel's guests, so he was pleasantly surprised to discover that on the whole they consisted of the same bankers, accountants, lawyers and other assorted pirates that he encountered from Monday to Friday. Charles Cottesmore made sure that he had a drink, and someone to talk to. Gawaine was swept off by Christabel.

"I gather your friend's going to put us all right about Father Thomas," his new companion said.

David murmured something.

His companion shot out a hand. "Andrew Danby," he introduced himself. "PCC Secretary. This is my wife Marjorie."

The woman with him smiled but said nothing. David wondered what a PCC was, and why it required a secretary, but he thought it would be gauche to ask. Instead, he introduced himself in turn, looking down at Danby, who was small, sinewy and vigorous, with a fringe of greying hair around a nut-brown bald head. "Did you know Father Thomas well?" he asked.

Danby shrugged. "As well as anybody here, I suppose,"

he replied. "And a bit better than I wanted to. You could say I had a grudge against him."

He brought out this remark so candidly that David was taken aback.

Danby twinkled with amusement. "Anyone will tell you," he went on, "so there's not much point in trying to hide it. He made a real nuisance of himself, didn't he, Marjorie?"

His wife agreed. David was wondering how to phrase the next obvious question, but Danby did not give him time to ask it.

"You see," he began, "we've got this rough bit of land attached to our garden. We've never used it for anything, not since the children used to keep their ponies there, and this developer approached me about it. Seems that he thought there was room to build a small house there – access to the road and everything – and he offered me a good price for it."

"We thought about it for a while," Marjorie went on, while David wondered what all this had to do with Father Thomas, "because of course we didn't want anything put up that would spoil the character of the village…"

Or the view from your windows, David supplied silently.

"You have to be very careful about developers." Danby took up the story again. "But it looked okay, and we talked it over with one or two people – Charles and Christabel, naturally – and the developer thought planning permission wouldn't be a problem, so the upshot was, we decided to sell."

He paused. David still wondered what all this had to do with Father Thomas.

"And then – guess what?"

"Can't imagine," David said.

"Father Thomas messed the whole deal up."

Danby paused again, as if once more inviting David to guess how the murdered priest could possibly have done that. David was starting to get irritated, but there was nothing to do except feed Danby with his next line. "How did he manage that?"

"He'd been looking at some old Church documents, and he discovered that there was a restriction on the land. You see, it was all Church land around here, once upon a time, including the land my house is built on, and this rough bit I wanted to sell. Apparently I couldn't resell it unless the Church approved, and the Church had the right of first refusal if the land came on the market again."

"That sounds quite a problem," David commented cautiously.

"Damn' inconvenient," Danby agreed. "You get these odd legal quirks from time to time, especially dealing with the Church. I went to my solicitor – Braid, he's here somewhere, a good chap – and he tried to sort something out, but Father Thomas wouldn't budge, and while the financial people in the diocese were working on it, my developer got fed up, withdrew his offer, and that was that."

He drained his gin and tonic. His challenging look showed David that a comment was expected.

"So you lost a good deal of money," David said.

"Damn' right I did. You wouldn't believe what a good building plot in Ellingwood is worth."

David thought that he probably would. "And now Father Thomas is dead…" he ventured.

"It might be easier to make the diocese see reason? Yes, it might. I've told all this to the police, of course."

David was a bit confused by his attitude. Danby had presented him with an excellent motive, with Father Thomas standing in the way of his making several thousand pounds, but he looked almost pleased as he told the story, as if he was enjoying the notoriety it gave him. Certainly he did not behave as if he thought anyone might seriously suspect him of doing Father Thomas in.

David decided on a frontal assault. "Were you in church the morning Father Thomas disappeared?" He was moderately pleased to see Danby's complacency waver.

"Yes, I was, as it happens. So was Marjorie."

"We always go to nine fifteen," his wife confirmed.

"Disappointed?" Danby asked, recovering himself with a chuckle. David tried to hide just how disappointed he was. "Never mind. You can't win 'em all."

David would have liked to pass all this on to Gawaine, but his friend had vanished somewhere. In any case, they could hardly discuss the possible guilt of Danby – or indeed of Mrs Danby, who looked quite healthy enough to wield a blunt instrument – in the presence of Christabel and her guests.

"Hey, Henry!" Danby exclaimed, gazing at someone behind David and beckoning vigorously. "Come over here and be grilled."

David turned to see a plump elderly man giving Danby an affronted look, then reluctantly edging his way towards them through the crowd. A woman – his wife, David supposed – followed him; she too was elderly, but tall and stringy while her husband was short and round. Both of them were sporting deep tans which suggested they had recently spent time somewhere more exotic than Surrey.

"This is Henry Hartley," Danby said, clapping the newcomer on his shoulder. "And his wife Beryl. Henry is our Church Treasurer," he added with a roguish wink at David.

Deciding that he really didn't like Danby, David shook hands and introduced himself. He felt a spark of interest in Henry Hartley, or more precisely in his position within the church. A Treasurer: might he not have had his hand in the till? And if Father Thomas had found out... Hartley might have an even better motive than Danby for wanting the vicar out of the way. It would be nice, David thought, to present Gawaine later with a brace of fully-fledged suspects.

"Pleased to meet you," Hartley grunted, sounding less than pleased. "And before you ask," he added, "I've no intention of being grilled. Christabel had no right to take such a high-handed step without consulting the PCC."

"Don't be ridiculous, Henry," his wife Beryl said. "Christabel is just doing her best to find out what happened. Goodness knows, the police aren't making much progress."

Before Hartley could protest any further, Christabel appeared, chivvying everyone into the dining room in search of food. David followed the crowd.

Lunch was laid out on a long table in the middle of the room. Someone thrust a plate into David's hand, but at first there were too many people around the table for him to start helping himself.

"What do you think of Christabel's 'tec?" a voice said somewhere behind David.

A snort was the response. "Not much. Feeble-looking sort of chap."

David deliberately didn't turn around to look for the source of the comments, hoping he might learn something. The second voice was elderly: David pictured a red face, a clipped moustache and a military bearing.

"Plays for the other team, d'you think?" the first voice asked.

"Shouldn't be at all surprised," the second voice responded. "Or his friend. Don't know what Christabel was thinking. We can do without that sort around here."

David stifled annoyance. It wasn't the first time someone had suggested that he and Gawaine might be a couple. He'd long ago come to the conclusion that it wasn't worth arguing. He would never convince anyone otherwise, if that was what they wanted to think.

Shrugging off the comments, he slid through the thinning crowd and scooped up a portion of coronation chicken.

When he moved out onto the patio, David was relieved to spot Gawaine sitting at one of the tables along with a tall, fair man and a dowdy little woman David assumed was his wife. Quickly he crossed the patio to join them.

"My dear David!" Gawaine rose and pulled out a chair for him. "This is Malcolm Braid and his sister Louise."

Sister, then, not wife, David thought, introducing himself as he sat down. *It's a pity her brother got all the looks in the family.*

"Mr Braid is the lay reader who took the service after Father Thomas disappeared," Gawaine went on. "He was just telling me about what happened when they found out he was missing."

Malcolm Braid nodded. "None of us could believe it," he said. "With the service just about to start... George Marshall was the first to notice, and he called me and Christabel. We searched, but there was no trace of him."

"Where did you look?" David asked.

"Everywhere we could look," Braid replied. "I went down the path to the vicarage, while Christabel searched the churchyard, and George dashed across to the hall. But Father Thomas wasn't anywhere."

"Stupid man!" Louise exclaimed.

Gawaine was looking thoughtful. "Did you go into the vicarage?"

"No, I tried the front and back doors, but they were locked. I rang the doorbell, but no one answered, and when I looked in the downstairs windows there was no sign of him."

"He might have been upstairs," David pointed out. "Suppose he was taken ill. He might have gone to lie down."

Braid gave a snort, as if he wasn't keen on that idea. "If he felt ill, all he had to do was open the vestry door and tell someone. Not just make off like that. Anyway, we checked later, and he wasn't there."

"And that doesn't explain how he came to be killed," Gawaine said, still looking mystified. "He would – "

He broke off as the Hartleys approached, carrying plates of food and looking around for spare seats. Most people were settled by then, and David thought that Henry Hartley seemed put out that the only vacant places were at Gawaine's table.

He doesn't want to talk to us. I wonder why.

Beryl Hartley, however, looked much more cheerful as she plonked her plate down on the table and herself on the chair Gawaine held out for her. Her husband followed, sitting down with a grunt that seemed to be his normal form of communication.

"What splendid tans you have," Louise said when introductions were over. "A cruise in the Bahamas, wasn't it?"

"That's right," Beryl replied. "It was wonderful."

Louise sighed. "I wish I could afford to do that. Mind you, dear, I'm surprised *you* could afford it, after you had that new extension built."

David saw her brother wince at this tactless comment, and forced himself not to glance at Gawaine. *The Church Treasurer, and with more money than he might be expected to have...* He noticed too that Henry Hartley was looking distinctly embarrassed, as if Louise had touched a nerve.

"It wasn't a problem," he said abruptly.

"It must have been a shock to come back and find all this trouble about Father Thomas," Gawaine said, smoothly moving the conversation on.

"Actually, we got back the night before he vanished," Beryl said. "But we were both so jetlagged that we didn't make it to church that Sunday. So we missed all the excitement."

This time David found it really difficult not to glance at Gawaine. The Hartleys might have been really nursing their jetlag, or they might have been murdering Father Thomas. *Motive and opportunity...*

"It's the kind of excitement I could do without," Malcolm Braid said. He shook his head, looking vaguely troubled. "I'm glad Christabel brought you in," he said to Gawaine. "How can we trust each other when we think that one of us must be a murderer?"

Louise gave a tinkling little laugh, though David thought there was little amusement in it. "Don't be ridiculous, Malcolm! How could it have been one of us? It must have been a...a tramp, or some sort of mugger..."

Braid sighed and patted his sister's hand. "You think that, Louise, if it makes you happier. But I can't agree with you, and I don't think the police will agree either."

Chapter Eight

Grant us by the same Spirit to have a right judgement in
all things.

The Collect for Whit Sunday

David was relieved to escape from Christabel's party and
stroll along the village street in the direction of the church.
The unseasonably warm day was drawing to a close; a
breeze had sprung up and dark clouds were massing in
the west.

"We're well out of that," David remarked after a while.

At David's side, Gawaine was silent, deep in thought.
A slight frown between his brows suggested he might have
a headache. He started as David spoke, as if his thoughts
had been a long way away.

"Sticky, certainly," he responded. "And full of people
who might have good reason to murder Father Thomas."

"Henry Hartley, for one," David said.

"The Church Treasurer." Gawaine nodded thoughtfully.
"Has he had his hand in the till? That's the question we
must ask ourselves, my dear David. He was certainly
embarrassed when Louise Braid made that remark about
affording his holiday."

"And no alibi," David added. "They say they were still
jetlagged after getting back the night before, but who's

to say they're telling the truth? And even jetlagged, you might manage to do in your vicar if it was urgent enough."

"That's true," Gawaine agreed, though David still thought his mind was elsewhere. "Though how urgent could it have been if they'd gone away on holiday and only just got back?"

"Surely the bishop could get the church accounts audited?" David suggested. "Or is it all done on trust?"

"Certainly not," Gawaine said, sounding shocked. "Church accounts are audited regularly. I'll phone the bishop's office tomorrow."

"Then there's Andrew Danby," David went on, describing the information he had gleaned about the failed development plans.

To his disappointment, Gawaine did not look impressed. "If the land really does, or did, belong to the Church," he said, "killing Father Thomas wouldn't make the slightest bit of difference. That development is never going to happen." He gestured vaguely. "Danby might have done it for revenge, but it's weak, David, very weak."

Reluctantly David had to agree. He had felt there was something subtly unpleasant about Andrew Danby, and he would have been delighted to put him on the spot. "Can you suggest anyone better?" he asked.

"There's John Bretton, the other churchwarden," Gawaine began. "He's the Head of Ellingwood Court, and Father Thomas managed to upset him seriously..."

David couldn't suppress a snort of amusement as he listened to the story of Father Thomas's influence on the prep school boys. "So Father Thomas got into trouble for actually doing his job?"

Gawaine blinked. "You could put it like that. Bretton would certainly want to stop him, if parents were threatening to remove their boys. But murdering the man seems a bit drastic, somehow."

"Was Bretton in church that morning?" David asked.

"No. He says he was working on the school accounts, though I don't know if he has any witnesses to that. And then there was Colonel Sutton," Gawaine went on. "Elderly and a trifle...reactionary, one might say. *He* approved of Father Thomas."

"Really?" David was surprised that anyone in Ellingwood had a good word to say for the late priest.

"Oh, yes. But for all the wrong reasons. Never mind refusing Communion to Ruth Reed. I gathered he would have been happier to see her whipped at the cart tail."

"Delightful," David murmured. "Still, it doesn't sound as if he would have a motive for murder, if he liked the guy."

"Unless that's what he wanted us to believe," Gawaine responded. "The Colonel doth protest too much, methinks. It might be a good idea to give him a little closer look." He paused thoughtfully, then added, "He mentioned someone called Chantal. He said that there wouldn't have been a fuss over her if Father Thomas had been in the parish."

"So that was something that happened a while back?"

"Two years ago, the Colonel said."

"And what was all the fuss about?"

"He wouldn't say," Gawaine replied, then added more thoughtfully, "I wonder if that's significant, that he wouldn't say."

"Maybe." David shrugged. "But it can't have anything to do with the murder if it happened before Father Thomas got here."

For a moment Gawaine didn't reply. He was inward-looking, as if, somewhere out of sight, tiny cogs were whirring energetically. David let them whir undisturbed. This wasn't the first time he had encountered Gawaine's instinctive ability to focus on a detail that to most people would appear completely unimportant. He felt a prickle of anticipation as he waited for the result.

But he was destined to be disappointed. Gawaine returned to reality and let out a long sigh.

"You're probably right," he responded to David's last remark. "But all the same, something is..." He gestured vaguely as if he was looking for the right word.

"Bugging you?" David suggested.

"Thank you, my dear David. Bugging me. Most expressive. Like an itch that I can't scratch. I think it might be a good idea to track down this Chantal, or at least find someone to tell us what happened."

"If you say so," David agreed, though he was still unconvinced that the mysterious Chantal would prove to be involved in their present problem.

Gawaine halted at the lychgate that led into the churchyard. "My dear David, all this may be very useful, but we're missing one important point."

"And that is?"

"Father Thomas might have been murdered in his vicarage, or in his church, or on the road on the way to the pub. So far we don't know where he was murdered, except that it wasn't in the priest's vestry. The one fact we do know

67

is that someone persuaded him to leave minutes before the Sunday morning service was due to start. What have we discovered that would make him do that?"

As David followed Gawaine through the lychgate he knew that the answer to that question was *nothing at all*.

Gawaine led the way to a bench in the shade of an ancient yew tree and disposed himself elegantly upon it. The day was growing cooler as the sun went down, and the breeze that brushed through the churchyard dislodged the first reddish-brown leaves from the beeches that bordered the road. From somewhere in the distance came the faint sound of a lawnmower.

"So," Gawaine said. "What did you discover this morning?"

David fished in his pocket and extracted a piece of paper where he had made a sketch map of the village. Gawaine bent over it with a faintly puzzled air.

"Here's the church," David said, coming to the rescue. "Here's the road that goes past it, with the church hall and the car park on the other side. Now here – " He traced it with his finger – "a lane goes off, called Church Lane, as you might expect, leading around the church and down to the vicarage. There are a couple of cottages at the top end, but the vicarage is the last house before the lane turns into a path going through woodland."

Gawaine nodded. "Interesting. I love those little trees you've drawn, my dear David. Very artistic."

"More to the point," David said, resisting an urge to prod Gawaine in the ribs, "the vicarage is quite isolated. Anything could go on down there, and you would never see it. Now," he went on, "in the other direction, the road past the church goes to the centre of the village. Village green, duck pond, Farrier's Arms, post office. Very picturesque. That's also the hub of the older houses, attractive, biggish gardens, owned by the likes of Christabel's little lot." Pulling out a pen, he added, "Let's add an X to mark Christabel's house, and we walked down this side street here."

He glanced at Gawaine to make sure his friend was following, then continued. "Okay, three more main roads lead off the village green. Down here are just houses that eventually peter out, and if you follow that road far enough you come to the Reeds' garden centre. Down here there's a parade of shops: an off-licence, newsagent, delicatessen, a little art gallery – "

"Oh?" Gawaine interrupted, looking interested. "Anything good in there?"

"How would I know?" David asked, exasperated. "Concentrate. Further down there, more houses, and a small school – not your Ellingwood Court, but the original village primary, by the look of it. And just beyond that the whole place opens up into a big modern development."

"Not a council estate, surely?" Gawaine asked. "Christabel would have had a fit."

David shook his head. "No, pretty upmarket. I'm sure you'd find some of Christabel's little lot down there, too. And the last road," he went on, pointing to it, "has more houses, a tea shop, another empty shop, a doctor's surgery, and the local solicitor's."

"That would be where Malcolm Braid has his lair," Gawaine murmured. He took the sketch map from David and examined it more closely. "I don't see Ellingwood Court here."

"I didn't notice it," David said. "It must be further out."

"I'd like to know where it is. How practical would it have been for John Bretton to have got to the church unobserved that Sunday morning?"

David fished in an inside pocket for his smartphone. "Nothing easier," he said, feeling the smugness of one who pulls a rabbit out of a hat. "Google Maps is your friend."

As he pressed the relevant buttons he was aware of Gawaine watching with all the concentration of a cat at a mousehole. "I could never get that to work," his friend said plaintively. "I always end up with a map of the world, or a huge enlargement of someone's back garden."

David flashed him a glance, wondering if that was true, aware as he was of how much Gawaine enjoyed pushing *his* buttons, and received only an innocent look in exchange. He said nothing, only concentrating until he had called up the relevant images.

"Very interesting," he said, holding the screen so that Gawaine could see it. "There's the church, and Church Lane, and the footpath that goes through the wood. It skirts a couple of fields, and comes out further down the road, just opposite – "

"Ellingwood Court!" Gawaine exclaimed, fixing David with an admiring look. "That means Bretton could have left the school, walked up the footpath and reached the church by way of the vicarage, without much risk of being spotted." He paused, his animation fading. "But did he?" he went on. "And if he did, what did he say to Father Thomas to persuade him to leave his vestry?"

David had no reply to that. It was the blank wall where their investigation had stalled. Father Thomas must have left the vestry of his own free will. And though David knew very little of the habits of vicars, he realised that only the most urgent news would have made him do that, just before the service was about to start.

Glancing at his watch, David realised that according to Gawaine it was almost time for their meeting with George Marshall, the sacristan. He had only a very hazy idea of what a sacristan did, but by the sound of it he was the man who could tell them exactly what had happened on the morning Father Thomas disappeared.

He heard footsteps on the gravel path that led around the church, then let out an exasperated sigh when the person who appeared was Seff Brown. For some reason she was looking frustrated, though she relaxed, smiling, when she saw Gawaine.

"My dear Persephone!" Gawaine rose to his feet and motioned her to his place on the bench.

Seff halted. "No, thanks, Gawaine, I won't stop. I went down to Ellingwood Court hoping for a word with John Bretton, but there's no one at home."

Gawaine gave a tight, feline smile. "There I can help you, my dear Persephone," he said, holding out David's sketch map. "X marks the spot. Christabel Cottesmore has been holding a lunch party. John Bretton was there, and a lot of other people who might be worthy of your attention."

David felt suddenly more cheerful at the thought of sicking Seff onto Christabel's guests. "It's starting to break up, though," he said, "so you'd better get a move on."

"I will. Thanks, I owe you one." Seff began moving smartly down the path to the lychgate, then stopped and turned back. "Come to think of it, I can pay you now. Look for Mrs Thorpe."

"Mrs Thorpe?" Gawaine echoed, looking puzzled. He glanced at David. "Has anyone mentioned – "

"Her name may not *be* Mrs Thorpe," Seff interrupted. "She was Mrs Thorpe in the church where I grew up, but every church has one. She's not in authority, and she's probably not on any committees. She's a flower-arranger, a hassock-mender, a cake-baker, and she knows *everything* that goes on. I haven't found her here yet, but I will. See you."

She turned and went off down the path, jauntily swinging her bag.

While Seff was speaking, a look of great enlightenment had dawned on Gawaine's face. "Of course! Mrs Thorpe... why didn't I think of that?"

"I don't see that it helps much," David said, unwilling to admit that Seff might have thought of something useful. "You can't go around asking all the old biddies in the congregation whether they're Mrs Thorpe."

Gawaine sighed. "Where is your subtlety, my dear David? I shall certainly – " He broke off as someone else appeared through the lychgate and came striding up the path. "Here's George Marshall. Maybe now we can start to find out what really happened."

Chapter Nine

...although the keeping or omitting of a Ceremony, in itself considered, is but a small thing; yet the wilful and contemptuous transgression and breaking of a common order and discipline is no small offence before God.

Of Ceremonies

David followed Gawaine into the church, past a door which stood open to reveal a set of bell-ropes and a narrow stair leading upwards, and down a side aisle. George Marshall led the way at a rapid pace and flung open a door at the far end. Entering, David found himself in a small room with a desk and a photocopier. Three of the four walls were taken up by built-in cupboards, and in the far corner was another door. Tall candles on stands, and various other bits of ecclesiastical paraphernalia took up more of the available space.

"This is the parish office," George announced. "And for want of a better, the servers' vestry."

"It must be very crowded in here when you're getting ready for a service," Gawaine said.

George sighed. "Tell me about it. And Father Thomas didn't make it any easier when he arrived."

"Oh? How was that?" David asked, wondering if here was someone else who was gunning for the late vicar.

"In Jim Trask's day, he never minded us storing our stuff in the priest's vestry, through there," George replied, nodding at the other door. "But Father Thomas liked to spend the time before the service praying and meditating, so we had to move everything into here. He was perfectly within his rights, of course," he added, "but it did cause a lot of inconvenience."

"May we see?" Gawaine asked, moving towards the inner door.

"Help yourself."

When David followed Gawaine inside he saw that the priest's vestry was an even smaller room, with more built-in cupboards, another desk, and a heavy old-fashioned safe in one corner. A crucifix was hanging on one wall, with a wooden kneeling desk in front of it.

"How did you manage about the safe?" Gawaine asked, speaking over his shoulder to George Marshall, who had remained in the outer vestry.

George appeared in the doorway. He had taken off his jacket and was buttoning himself into a long black cassock. "We couldn't move it; it's bolted to the wall," he replied. "So woe betide me if I wasn't here early enough to take out the Communion silver before Father Thomas got here. He would turn up at ten to nine on the dot, and after that the connecting door had to stay shut."

"Hmm…" Gawaine blinked thoughtfully and drifted across to yet one more door, a heavy oak affair with iron bolts drawn across. "This leads outside?" he asked.

George nodded. "Let me show you."

He fished in his trouser pocket, drew out a bunch of keys and opened the door, drawing the bolts back with a loud scraping noise.

David exchanged a surprised look with Gawaine. "It wasn't locked like that when Father Thomas disappeared? Or did he let his murderer in?"

"No," George replied. "I would unbolt it when I first arrived. Father Thomas had his own key to let himself in. After that, while the church is in use the door has to stay unlocked, because it's a fire exit."

"So anyone could have walked in," Gawaine murmured.

Standing in the doorway, he looked out. Over his shoulder David could see a path leading through the churchyard as far as an iron gate in a wall of weathered stone. Beyond it, through a screen of trees and bushes he could just make out the walls and roof of a red-brick building.

"I take it that's the vicarage," Gawaine said, venturing a few paces down the path.

David followed. As he gazed around, he realised how isolated they were. The bulk of the church hid them from the main road, and the vicarage was the only house in view. It would be easy for someone to approach up the path from the vicarage without being seen.

"This door is the only other access to the church?" Gawaine asked, his thoughts clearly running along the same lines.

"Apart from the main south door, yes," George replied. "The other door at the west end only leads to the bell tower."

"And no one would try to get in here through the church," Gawaine said, returning to the vestry. "They would certainly have been spotted."

While George Marshall closed the outer door again, Gawaine stood still, gazing around. After a moment he picked up a framed photograph that stood on the desk, frowning thoughtfully as he gave it a closer look.

"What's that?" David asked, joining him.

The photograph showed a group of white, wooden buildings, lit by brilliant sunshine. The one in the centre had a cross fixed to the outside; David assumed it was a church. A group of Africans in traditional dress were posed in front of it. In the middle of the group was a single European, in a white cassock and clerical collar.

"That's Father Thomas," George Marshall said. "He told me it was taken at the festival for the dedication of the church."

"*That's* Father Thomas?" David was astonished. He had imagined the late vicar as an older man with a sombre, even threatening look as he whipped his parishioners into order. This man was no more than forty, long and lanky with a deep tan and a shock of bright red hair. He was grinning cheerfully at the camera.

"He did good work out there, by all accounts," George went on. "As well as the church, he got funding for a clinic and a school, and a well with an irrigation system to bring clean water to the village." He sighed. "I'm sure he was a lot happier out there than he was here in Ellingwood."

"He came back for his health?" Gawaine asked.

"Yes. Not that it did him much good."

Gawaine looked distressed at this macabre thought, and returned the photograph to the desk. A moment later he straightened up, clearly trying to push the idea to the back of his mind.

"Tell us about that Sunday morning," he said. "I suppose Father Thomas was at your early service?"

George Marshall shook his head. "We used to have an eight o'clock and a ten, but hardly anyone came to the eight o'clock, so we combined both services into the nine fifteen."

"So that was the last time Father Thomas was seen," Gawaine said. "I take it he was seen? You didn't all just assume that he was here?"

David perked up at that question. So far the investigation was foundering on the problem of why Father Thomas would have left the vestry so close to the start of the service. It would make life a good deal easier if he hadn't been there at all.

"Oh, he was seen," George Marshall said.

"How, if you had to keep the connecting door shut?" David asked, reluctant to abandon this attractive new theory.

"Well, you remember I told you that we had to move all our stuff out of the priest's vestry into here? We all found it difficult to get used to, so now and again items would migrate to their old places. On that particular Sunday, when it was time to light the candles, we couldn't find the taper." George pointed to a long wooden rod where it stood in a corner; at one end it had a wax taper fixed into a thin brass tube, and a conical brass snuffer. "Eventually we realised it must have been put away in the priest's vestry."

"Awkward. What did you do?" Gawaine asked.

"One of my acolytes slipped in and got it. She said Father Thomas had his back to her, and never even noticed she'd been there. We all heaved a huge sigh of relief!"

"And you're sure she's telling the truth?" David persisted. "She's not saying it to make herself important?"

George Marshall gave him a frosty stare. "Katie Rook – Jennifer's eldest – is my most reliable server. If she says she saw Father Thomas, then she saw him. Besides, she told me at the time, long before we knew there was going to be a problem." Turning to Gawaine, he added, "If you want to talk to her – with her parents' permission, naturally – I can fix it up, but I promise you there's no need."

"Maybe later," Gawaine said. "But for the present I think we can take it that was the last time anyone saw Father Thomas alive. What time was it, exactly?"

"Exactly?" George grinned. "That's a bit of a tall order. But I can nail it down pretty precisely. The acolytes would normally start to light the candles at five past nine, so give Katie a minute or two to look for the taper…say six or seven minutes past nine."

"And what happened after that?"

George shrugged. "Not much. When it was time for the service to start and Father Thomas hadn't appeared, I put my head round the door to have a look. His chasuble, his amice and his alb were thrown over the back of his chair and the outer door was open, but there was no sign of him. I don't understand why he would have left like that, without a word to anyone," he added. "I thought he was more responsible than that."

"And you hadn't heard anything unusual?" David asked.

"Not a whisper."

"Spirited away by the fairies…" Gawaine murmured.

"He might as well have been," said George. "But I think we can take it that it wasn't the fairies who hit him over the head and dumped his body on the Downs."

Chapter Ten

…the bishop of the diocese […] by his discretion shall take order for the quieting and appeasing of the same.

Concerning the Service of the Church

"I suppose you'll have to leave tonight," Gawaine said as he and David crossed the road to the church hall car park where David had left his car.

"Not unless you're throwing me out," David replied.

"But tomorrow is Monday." Gawaine sounded faintly nervous. David realised that only the pricking of his conscience was making him have this conversation. "Don't you have to go to work?"

Sadly, yes, I do. The advertising agency which owned David's time from Monday to Friday offered nothing as intriguing as the problem of Father Thomas's murder.

"I've every intention of going to work," he responded. "I'm going to commute. Plenty of people do it."

"Oh, but – " Gawaine started to object, then fell silent.

"Look," David went on, glancing swiftly aside to see Gawaine's face set in a worried expression. "I go to work, you head for Ellingwood with your deerstalker and your magnifying glass, and in the evening we discuss what you've found."

Gawaine's worry dissolved into reluctant amusement.

"Deerstalker and magnifying glass? If only... No, I see myself more as a cat," he added ruefully. "Hunting for information, and dropping my prey at your feet like undigested mouse gobbets."

"Yuck."

"Yuck indeed." Gawaine sighed. "I have the feeling, my dear David, that most of the information I turn up in Ellingwood will be even less salubrious than mouse gobbets."

David got into the car, waited for Gawaine to settle himself in the passenger seat, and drove off, thinking affectionately of the person who would use the word 'salubrious' in everyday conversation.

On the following morning David departed for London, still insisting that he intended to commute to work until the investigation was over. He left Gawaine feeling guilty, as he always did, at interfering in his friend's life.

When David had gone, and morning coffee had done its work, Gawaine telephoned the bishop. This time the personal assistant passed him straight through.

"I think we ought to meet," the bishop said, before Gawaine could raise the matter of the church accounts. "I'm coming over in your direction this afternoon. Would that suit you?"

"Certainly," Gawaine replied. "Come for tea. Around four?"

With that satisfactorily arranged he put the phone down and went to find Mrs Summers, to ask her to bake a cake fit for a bishop.

Meanwhile there was the rest of the day to fill in, and

though Gawaine would have much preferred to attend to his garden, or work on the paper on Cimabue that he was gradually knitting together, he recognised with a sigh that his time had to be spent in pursuing the truth about Father Thomas's death. Even more reluctantly, he accepted that it was high time he made contact with the police.

Driving into Ellingwood, he spotted a couple of police cars in the church car park, and turned in to stop beside them. The main doors of the church hall were locked, but further investigation round the back revealed another door leading to a tiny lobby with a large bare room beyond it. Gawaine realized that this must be the backstage area of the main hall.

Now the room was filled with trestle tables where police officers were bending earnestly over computers, in the midst of a scatter of phones, plastic coffee cups and chocolate biscuit wrappers. At the far end was a large whiteboard with various scribblings, too far away for Gawaine to make out, and a blown-up photograph of Father Thomas. Gawaine regarded the untidy shock of red hair and the cheerful expression, and realised that he would have enjoyed talking to this man.

One police officer was pacing about between the tables, a mobile phone clamped to his ear. When he spotted Gawaine he finished the call abruptly and strode over to him.

"And you are?" he barked.

Gawaine narrowly avoided flinching. The officer, in his shirt-sleeves, was slightly overweight, broad-shouldered, with thinning dark hair combed straight back. Gawaine could have imagined him in the front line of a rugby scrum, if he had ever so far forgotten himself as to watch a rugby match.

Introducing himself, he added, "I believe the bishop..?"

"Yes, so the Chief Constable tells me," the officer interrupted. "And we'd better get this straight right away: I don't want you here, but it looks as if I have to put up with you."

Gawaine shrugged elegantly. "There I have to agree with you. I don't want to be here either."

The officer looked somewhat mollified. "DCI Ferris," he said, reaching out to take Gawaine's hand in a grip almost as ferocious as Colonel Sutton's. "So let's get down to the nitty-gritty. What can I do for you – or more to the point, what can you do for me?"

He gestured Gawaine to one of the plastic chairs beside a table, and sat down beside him. "Coffee?" he asked.

Gawaine suppressed a shudder and declined gracefully. "I'm sorry that I haven't much information for you at present," he began. "I assume you've spoken to George Marshall about the way that Father Thomas vanished?"

"Yes. And one of my women officers went to interview the girl who saw him in the vestry. She was impressed by her: she seemed to be a straight-forward, honest little kid." Ferris hesitated, then added, "We did a house-to-house around the village. No one admits to seeing Father Thomas after he left the church. Though he did send a text a few minutes later."

"A text?" Gawaine's mind flitted to the academic, until he realised that Ferris must be talking about a mobile phone.

"Yes, to Braid, the lay reader," Ferris replied. "Sent at ten past nine from the vicarage garden, or just possibly from the lane outside the gate."

"It didn't say where he was going?" Gawaine asked, without much hope of a useful answer.

"No. Just said sorry, and would Braid take the evening service."

"So that would imply Father Thomas went to the vicarage," Gawaine mused, "and then maybe left in a car, or by the footpath that leads down to Ellingwood Court. Or he was killed in the vicarage."

DCI Ferris shook his head emphatically. "No. He was definitely not killed there. Or in the vicarage garden. And not where he was found, either. I can't help but think that if we knew where he was killed, we might get a better handle on who killed him."

"True," Gawaine agreed. "Would it be all right with you, Chief Inspector, if I take a look around the vicarage?"

"Be my guest," Ferris replied. To Gawaine's relief he was sounding, if not friendly, at least no longer hostile. "We're all done there. You can get the key from one of that lot at the church. Now – anything else? Because I have an investigation to run."

Gawaine realised that this was the time to be succinct. "What can you tell me about the body?"

"Well, you can imagine the state it was in, after a fortnight in the wood on the downs." Gawaine briefly closed his eyes, trying hard not to imagine it. "Death was from a blow on the head," Ferris went on. "Two separate blows, to be accurate, from something smooth and round…maybe the size and shape of a doorknob.

Obviously not an actual doorknob," he finished, clearly demonstrating a low opinion of Gawaine's intelligence.

"And you don't have the weapon?" Gawaine asked.

"We do not."

"And is there any indication when he was killed? I suppose after a fortnight it's hard to be really precise."

"You'd be surprised," Ferris said with a grin. "Stomach contents showed a partly digested meal, involving eggs and bread. I'd guess he had eggs on toast for breakfast about an hour before he was killed."

"So it happened soon after he vanished from the vestry..." Gawaine felt a definite stirring of interest. Whatever had lured Father Thomas away must have been cataclysmic, if he had been dead so soon after.

Frowning thoughtfully, he wondered if there was anything else he ought to ask. DCI Ferris was stirring restlessly, a phone had just started ringing across the room, and clearly Gawaine was within seconds of being kicked out.

"What was he wearing when he was found?" he asked.

Ferris waved a hand irritably. "That long black thing that vicars wear..."

"That would be a cassock," Gawaine put in.

"A cassock, yeah. And under it a black shirt, dog-collar, the usual trousers, underwear, socks, shoes... Nothing in the trouser pockets except a handkerchief."

Gawaine's interest sharpened. "So no identification?"

"No, but given his get-up, that's not really surprising. No jacket, so no wallet."

"And no keys? No mobile phone?"

"No," said Ferris. "His keys were found later, in the

84

vestry. I'd guess that the murderer removed the phone and anything else that might have identified him. But we ID'd him fast enough from the description we were given when he went missing. Not many red-haired vicars in these parts."

"Interesting…" Gawaine murmured. *It would make more sense to remove his cassock and his collar as well if he didn't want him identified.* "I suppose you've tried tracking his phone?" he asked.

"Not possible, if it's switched off." Ferris stood up. "Or if it's smashed and at the bottom of the nearest river, which would be my guess. Now, if there's nothing else…"

"No, you've been very helpful, Chief Inspector," Gawaine said, also rising. "And if I find out anything, I'll be sure to let you know."

"You do that, Mr St Clair," Ferris responded, holding out a business card. "Ring this number. But I won't hold my breath."

The bishop stretched out his long length in a basket chair in Gawaine's conservatory, beneath a cascade of white bougainvillaea. Gawaine deposited a tray of Earl Grey and apricot fruit loaf on the small table beside him, and took the chair opposite.

"So," the bishop said as Gawaine poured the tea. "Are you making any progress?"

"Of a sort," Gawaine replied, hoping that was true. "I'd rather not name any names at this stage. But I think it might be a good idea to get the church accounts audited."

"Really?" The bishop's brows rose. "Interesting. I can certainly put that through for you."

"I'm not making any accusations," Gawaine added hastily.

"Of course not. But I can see that the accounts might be an...area of concern." The bishop accepted a cup of tea and a wedge of fruit loaf. "Father Thomas's background," he went on briskly. "He came originally from the north of England; he read theology at Leeds and studied for the priesthood at Mirfield. Once ordained he did a curacy at the Priory Church in Lancaster, and then went out to Sierra Leone with an Anglican project to develop upcountry villages. He did rather well out there," the bishop finished with an emphatic nod.

"But his health gave way?"

The bishop nodded again, while masticating a mouthful of fruit loaf. "Excellent cake, Gawaine. Yes, Father Thomas had a bad dose of malaria, and being malaria, as I'm sure you know, it keeps recurring. He stuck it out for a while, but finally the project organisers told him he had to pack up and come back to Britain."

"He must have been upset about that," Gawaine observed.

"Very. He felt he had a call to be out there. But Sierra Leone's loss was my gain, as Father Thomas became available just after Jim Trask retired from St Paul's and I had to decide what to do about the parish."

Something about the way the bishop said that puzzled Gawaine. "But Father Thomas was just filling in there, wasn't he?"

"Officially," the bishop replied. "But privately I can tell you I fully intended that he should take over the incumbency."

"Really?" Gawaine practically spilled his tea in surprise, and quickly set the cup down. "I remember Christabel Cottesmore told me that Father Thomas was putting in an application, but surely he'd made himself too unpopular? The churchwardens would never have appointed him."

The bishop gave Gawaine a slightly feral smile. "I can assure you, Gawaine, that I would be perfectly within my rights to over-ride the churchwardens if I felt it necessary."

Gawaine wasn't sure what to say. He hadn't realized that the bishop could do that, and his statement opened up a whole new area of the investigation.

While he dithered, the bishop leaned back in his chair, placed his fingertips precisely together and gazed up at the bougainvillaea – or possibly at the heavens that lay beyond it.

"You're not stupid, Gawaine," he said after a moment. "I'm sure you must have realised that all is not well at St Paul's." He paused for a murmur of agreement from Gawaine and continued, "Jim Trask was a good man, but he should have retired five years before he did. The work of the parish became too much for him, and he let too much control slip into the hands of the churchwardens, and to a lesser extent of the PCC. This is in the strictest confidence, mind you," he added, sitting up again and fixing Gawaine with a stare from frosty grey eyes.

"Of course," Gawaine responded, mentally reserving the right to discuss it all with David, who would never dream of passing on a word of it.

"What St Paul's needs," the bishop went on, "is a man – or, indeed, a woman – with enough clout to take back control, and return St Paul's to the worship of our Lord

Jesus Christ…as opposed to the worship of material goods and respectability, which is where the parish stands at the moment. Thomas Coates was not a man to be easily intimidated. He seemed like – and probably was – the answer to prayer."

"Not any more," Gawaine said soberly. "But would it have worked?" he asked. "Wasn't Father Thomas too… too rigid? I understand what you're saying, but surely you didn't approve of his refusing Communion to Ruth Reed?"

"Of course I didn't," the bishop told him. "And if necessary I would have sorted it out, but Mrs Reed seemed happy enough to take herself off to St John's. I discussed the whole matter with Dan Stafford, who's vicar there." He paused, with another glance upwards at the snowy fountain of bougainvillaea, then continued, "Father Thomas tended to see things in extreme terms of right and wrong, no doubt because of his experience in Africa. But you and I know that there are many grey areas. I was fully aware that he would have needed guidance, and I was prepared to give it. I firmly believe that he would have developed into a man of strong and profound spirituality."

Gawaine was silent, contemplating how all that potential had been destroyed by a blow to the head with a blunt instrument.

"May he rest in peace," the bishop said, and crossed himself. He let the silence continue for a little longer, then let out a gusty sigh. "I expect you'll want to know about Father Thomas's family."

"He had family?" Gawaine wasn't sure why this should surprise him, but until now he had thought of Father Thomas as solitary. After all, the police had needed

Christabel to identify his body, and though she had mentioned a brother, she hadn't seemed sure whether he existed or not.

"Oh, yes. His parents are dead, but he has an older brother and sister. My secretary got in touch with them to tell them what had happened, and they came down from Manchester at the weekend. They're staying in a hotel in Guildford until the police release the body. Will you need to talk to them?"

"I suppose I should," Gawaine responded, though inwardly he shrank from confronting the family's grief. He supposed there would be grief.

"That can be arranged. And of course there's the matter of Father Thomas's will."

"His will?" Gawaine's mind was reeling from the pressure of all the new information that was being pumped into it. "I assumed that what he had to leave would be negligible…not a motive for murder."

"Don't you believe it," the bishop said. "His brother and sister run a business in Manchester, importing silks, rugs and so on from the Far East. I gather that they do very well out of it, and Father Thomas owned thirty per cent of the shares. It'll be very interesting to find out who he left them to."

"It will indeed," Gawaine said faintly.

Chapter Eleven

…man is very far gone from original righteousness, and is of his own nature inclined to evil.

Article ix

On the following morning Gawaine was feeling alone and a little disconsolate. He had discussed his new information with David over dinner the night before, and David had latched immediately onto the startling news that Father Thomas had owned a good proportion of a thriving business.

"We need know who benefits," David said. "And that means looking at his will. Do you know who his solicitor is?"

Gawaine shook his head. "I doubt it's Malcolm Braid," he said. "Father Thomas hadn't been here long enough. The bishop said he would ask Father Thomas's brother and sister. They must know something about it."

David snorted. "They might know a whole lot about it. A brother or a sister would be far more likely to get Father Thomas out of that vestry than just some random bloke showing up. If they thought of a good excuse."

"True. I shall have to meet them," Gawaine had responded. "Though I can't say I'm looking forward to it."

But now David had departed for London to earn his honest crust, leaving Gawaine to set out for Ellingwood again. With no further word from the bishop, he had decided that the best thing to do would be to tackle the vicarage, and drove to Christabel's to pick up the keys.

He had telephoned ahead, so that when Christabel opened her door to him she had the keys in her hand.

"Here you are," she said. "Don't forget to bring them back. And leave everything down there as you find it."

Gawaine murmured assent.

"Have you found out anything?" Christabel asked as she handed the keys over. "This is all becoming intolerable."

"These things take time," Gawaine told her, "though I think I'm making progress." He was unwilling to share any of his suspicions with Christabel; passing on speculations about people who might be totally innocent was not part of his remit.

Christabel's only response was a poorly-suppressed snort.

"There is one thing you might be able to help me with," Gawaine went on. "What can you tell me about a woman named Chantal?"

Christabel's gaze was suddenly fixed, her eyes narrowed in suspicion. "Her? Who's been telling you about her?" When Gawaine did not reply, she added, "She set up a business here, but it was a long time ago. It can't possibly have anything to do with Father Thomas's murder."

"What sort of business?" Gawaine asked.

"A beauty salon, if you please! And a massage parlour. And we all know what *that* means."

Gawaine blinked. "We do?" he asked, in the faint hope that Christabel would come straight out with what she was implying.

He was destined to be disappointed.

"Don't pretend to be stupid, Gawaine," Christabel snapped. "In any case, it was all quite unsuitable for Ellingwood. She closed down and left. And now, if you don't mind, I have things to do."

Gawaine had barely time to step back before she shut the door in his face. He was thinking hard as he drove off and parked once again in the church car park.

There's something here that I'm not seeing. I need to find out more about Chantal.

Shelving the problem for the time being, Gawaine crossed the road and passed through the lychgate, intending to skirt around the church and take the footpath down to the vicarage, following in the – presumed – footsteps of Father Thomas. But as he passed the main south door his curiosity was aroused by a buzzing sound coming from inside the building. He slipped through the porch, opened the door quietly and put his head round it.

The buzzing sound – louder now – came from a vacuum cleaner, which an elderly woman was busily pushing up the main aisle. She wore an old-fashioned flowered pinny over a brown skirt and a hand-knitted cardigan, and her tight grey curls bobbed in rhythm with the movement of the cleaner.

Gawaine was about to withdraw as silently as he had come when something stirred at the back of his mind. What was it Seff had said? He slid inside, closed the door behind him, and waited until the woman had reached the altar steps and turned around, vigorously vacuuming her way back towards him.

While he waited, Gawaine noticed the churchwardens'

rods of office that were affixed to pew-ends about half way to the front of the church. He especially noticed the brass ornaments on top: smooth and round, about the size of a doorknob.

But surely someone would have noticed if one went missing…

Gawaine dismissed that to be considered later as the elderly woman came into range. He stepped forward. "Mrs Thorpe?"

The woman started and cut off her machine. "You gave me such a turn!" she exclaimed. "Why do you want to creep up on people like that?"

"I'm sorry, I – "

"And my name's not Thorpe. It's Prestwick. Mrs Prestwick."

"Good morning. I'm – "

"I know who you are," Mrs Prestwick said, giving him a beady look. "You're this fellow Christabel Cottesmore brought in to find out about Father Thomas. Well, I'm sure I wish you the best of luck."

"You liked Father Thomas?" Gawaine asked, managing to get a word in, and encouraged to find someone who was happy to have him around. He hoped that Mrs Prestwick had better reasons for liking Father Thomas than Colonel Sutton had expressed.

"He was a decent young man – though he could be stupid, just like all men," Mrs Prestwick replied. "I said to his face that he was wrong about Ruth Reed, but would he listen?" Her tone darkened. "I could have told him, there are people round here who shouldn't be coming up to take the holy bread and wine, much worse than poor Ruth."

"Really?" Gawaine said, becoming more interested by the second. "But you didn't tell Father Thomas about them?"

Mrs Prestwick sniffed. "I did not. It's not my place to gossip."

Gawaine was well aware that at this juncture a gentleman would have bidden Mrs Prestwick good morning and continued on his way. Sadly, remaining a gentleman at all times was a luxury he couldn't afford.

"But now that Father Thomas is dead...?" he murmured.

Mrs Prestwick repeated the sniff. "You might ask that Andrew Danby what he gets up to, sneaking down to the headmaster's house while John Bretton is in school. I do for Stella Bretton, and the goings-on you wouldn't believe!"

"Fascinating."

"It's Marjorie Danby who has the money, you know," Mrs Prestwick continued with relish. "He was no more than a jumped-up bank clerk before he retired. Father Thomas could have put a cat in among those pigeons, all right!"

"But he didn't know?"

"Well, seeing as nothing happened, no he didn't. But it wouldn't have been long, you mark my words. And that's not all. There's that Colonel Sutton, always eyeing up the Young Wives' group, and him old enough to be their dad, if not their granddad."

Gawaine suppressed a shudder. "Really?"

"Not that I think he's ever *done* anything," Mrs Prestwick went on. "But it's still not decent, is it? 'If thine eye offend thee, pluck it out.' That's what the Good Book says."

"Quite."

"And what about Louise Braid, always making up to the doctor?" Mrs Prestwick put the question like a challenge, as if she expected Gawaine to have an answer.

"What about her?" Gawaine asked, all at sea.

"Oh, you won't have met Doctor Jerrold," Mrs Prestwick went on. "He doesn't come to church. Louise Braid works as his receptionist, and she's always smarming around him, Doctor Jerrold this and Doctor Jerrold that. It makes me sick. As if he'd ever look at her, and him a married man with two little kiddies."

"You 'do for' the Jerrolds as well, I suppose?" Gawaine said.

"You suppose right. A very nice woman, Amy Jerrold, and how she puts up with that Louise I do not know. And now I have to get on. I'm due at the Cottesmores at eleven."

"Then I won't keep you much longer," Gawaine said as Mrs Prestwick turned back to her vacuum cleaner. "But I need to ask you, have you ever noticed one of the churchwardens' staves not being in its proper place?"

Mrs Prestwick swung round to stare at the brass-topped rods. "I can't say I have…" she said. "Here, do you think it was one of them did for Father Thomas?"

"It's possible."

"Well, I never! I give them a good polish regular, like I do all the brass, and I never thought…"

Gawaine winced at the thought of what Mrs Prestwick might have destroyed with her duster and polish. "I'll have a word with the police," he said. "And please don't touch them again until they've been checked."

"I won't. I'm not stupid. And now, if you don't mind, I've work to do. I'm going to be late at the Cottesmores if I'm not careful."

She touched a foot control and her machine roared into life again.

"Oh, and one last question." Gawaine raised his voice over the noise. "What can you tell me about a woman called Chantal?"

"*Her*?" Mrs Prestwick glared at him. "The less said about *her*, the better." Immediately contradicting herself, she went on, "Chantal Dupont, she called herself, though if you ask me, she was no more French than I am."

Again Gawaine felt the flicker of interest that told him there might be more to discover, even if the 'fuss', as Colonel Sutton had called it, had happened two years before.

"Can you tell me where to find her?" he asked.

"I can not. She doesn't live here no more. I don't know where she went, and I don't want to know." She swivelled her vacuum cleaner around. "That's all over and done with."

"Thank you." Gawaine accepted that the interview was over, even though he might have been tempted to ask if Mrs Prestwick had any interesting revelations to make about Christabel. But he knew he had lost her sympathy, and besides, he wasn't sure he wanted to know the answer to that. "If you think of anything else relevant, please let me know."

"I'll do that," Mrs Prestwick said, and zoomed off into the side chapel.

No one wants to talk about Chantal, Gawaine thought as he left the church. *Not Christabel, not Mrs Prestwick.*

*Not even Colonel Sutton, although he brought her name up.
I wonder...*

Once again putting Chantal to the back of his mind, Gawaine continued around the side of the church and down the footpath that led from the door of the priest's vestry to the gate into the vicarage garden. He took his time, scanning the path and the surrounding vegetation, although he wasn't sure what he was looking for.

Sherlock Holmes, he told himself, would have found a telltale footprint, a sprinkling of cigar ash, or a mysterious thread caught on a twig, but there was nothing like that to be seen here. And if there had been, the police would have already found it.

Reaching the iron gate in the wall, Gawaine let himself into the vicarage garden and picked his way through the shrubbery until he reached the house. It was built of weathered red brick, and the woodwork could have done with a lick of paint. Weeds had encroached on the path that led around the side of the house.

When Gawaine reached the front, he halted in surprise. The gate to Church Lane was open, and a gleaming black car was parked in the drive. Listening, Gawaine thought that he could hear subdued movement and voices from inside.

Nervously he hesitated. Christabel hadn't told him that anyone from the congregation intended to visit the vicarage. Could there be thieves in there, or even the murderer? Then he gave himself a shake, and told himself to stop being stupid. Thieves could hardly expect to find anything in an unoccupied vicarage, and anything the murderer wanted could have been removed weeks ago.

Gawaine walked up to the front door and instead of using Christabel's key, rang the bell. There was a pause, then approaching footsteps, and the door was opened.

Standing in the doorway was a small, slim woman, dressed neatly and practically in jeans and a sweater. Her hair was swept back into a sleek French pleat, but its flaming red colour told Gawaine who she must be. Her face looked white and drawn, as if she had been sleeping badly.

"Yes?" she said pleasantly.

Before Gawaine could reply, a man loomed up behind her. He too had red hair, though his was peppered with grey. He had a watchful look: not hostile, but as though he didn't welcome the interruption.

"What can we do for you?" he asked.

"I'm sorry to interrupt," Gawaine began, feeling awkward. He wasn't ready for this encounter yet. "I think you must be Father Thomas's brother and sister?"

"That's right." The woman answered readily; she was much the more friendly of the two. "This is Richard Coates, and I'm Susan Cox."

Gawaine introduced himself, and was relieved to see that Richard Coates relaxed, his wariness vanishing. "The bishop told us about you," he said. "Come in."

He ushered Gawaine into a small square hall, and from there into the sitting room of the vicarage. It was unfurnished except for a couple of armchairs and a coffee table.

"I'm so sorry about what happened to your brother," Gawaine said. "It must have been a terrible shock."

Susan nodded. "We were so pleased to get him back from Africa. It was such a worry, having him out there. We never thought…" Her voice shook and she turned away.

"You read about this kind of thing in the paper, but you never imagine it'll happen to anyone you know," her brother said. "All we want now is to find out who did it. So if we can help you in any way, just ask."

"I came to have a look around," Gawaine explained. "But if it's not convenient…"

"No, it's fine." Susan had recovered herself. "The police told us it would be all right to come and pack up Tom's personal things, but we've barely started; we've only just arrived. We can wait until you're done."

"Provided it doesn't take too long," Richard added.

"It won't," Gawaine promised. "I'll start upstairs, if that's all right with you."

He was glad to escape, wishing he could have examined the place alone, but thankful that at least Father Thomas's property was still there.

The vicarage had three bedrooms, but only one of them was furnished, with a single bed, a bedside cabinet and a *prie-dieu* set against one wall with a crucifix nailed above it. The built-in wardrobe contained one suit, a linen jacket and a scanty collection of shirts, socks and underwear.

Feeling uncomfortably nosy, Gawaine went through the pockets and located Father Thomas's wallet inside the jacket. It held a couple of ten pound notes, an expired return half of a ticket to Manchester – visiting his brother and sister, Gawaine supposed – and the photograph of a young African woman.

Gawaine examined this with a stirring of interest. Nothing he had heard so far suggested that Father Thomas was the sort of man who would be carrying pictures of women next to his heart. But there was no reason, he reflected, why the title of 'Father' should convey an intention of remaining permanently celibate. The woman was attractive, gazing out of the photograph with a lively, cheerful expression.

She was happy when that was taken…

Replacing the photograph in the wallet and the wallet in the jacket, Gawaine checked the bedside cabinet, where he found a Bible and a pair of reading glasses, then quickly glanced around the bathroom. There was nothing to see there, only basic toiletries and a pack of prescription medication which Gawaine assumed was for Father Thomas's malaria.

Heading downstairs, he found nothing of interest in the kitchen or sitting room, and the dining room was completely bare. Two more doors remained in the hall: the first led to a coat cupboard where an anorak and a heavy black cloak were hanging. A quick search of both revealed nothing except a piece of string and a ball-point pen in one of the pockets of the anorak. Disappointed, he realised that he had hoped to track down the missing mobile phone somewhere the police had failed to discover it.

Meanwhile he could hear voices coming from behind the last door; Gawaine tapped on it before entering.

This room had evidently been Father Thomas's study. Built-in bookshelves lined one wall, though only half a shelf was filled with books. A scrubbed pine table served as a desk, with paper and pens scattered over it. A fat commentary on the Gospel of St Luke lay open with a page of scribbled notes beside it: an embryo sermon, Gawaine deduced.

Susan was beginning to sort through the books, though she stood back when Gawaine appeared. "Do you want to look at these before I pack them?" she asked.

Gawaine nodded thanks, and stepped up to the shelf. Most of the books were theological, except for a few paperbacks: novels and poems by West African writers. Gawaine flipped through each book in turn, but nothing incriminating fell out, nothing at all except for a couple of prayer cards.

As he examined the commentary, Gawaine noticed a name written in the front: Malcolm Braid. "This doesn't seem to have belonged to Father Thomas," he said, showing the flyleaf to Susan. "Malcolm Braid is the lay reader here."

"Tom must have borrowed it," Susan said, sounding slightly harassed.

"I can take it back, if you like," Gawaine said, thinking that he wouldn't object to another conference with Malcolm Braid, preferably without his tactless sister.

"Oh, would you? That would be such a help!"

"We'd better get on, Sue," her brother said, beginning to pack the books into a cardboard carton which stood on the floor. To Gawaine he added, "Was there anything else?"

"There is one thing." Gawaine felt suddenly nervous again, but knew that he had to grasp this opportunity before these valuable informants decamped to Manchester. "Can you tell me anything about Father Thomas's will?"

Richard exchanged a glance with Susan; she gave a tiny nod. "We can tell you everything about Tom's will," Richard replied.

Gawaine had expected annoyance at the question, and was thankful that both Richard and Susan seemed willing to co-operate. "The bishop said that Father Thomas owned a share in your business," he said.

"That's right," Richard told him. "Our father started the firm, and that's how he left it. Forty per cent to me, and thirty per cent each to Tom and Sue."

"Tom's will divides it between us," Susan went on. "With the understanding that we pay the income to the Nazareth Trust."

"That's the outfit that Tom worked for in Africa," Richard explained. "Most of his income went there when he was alive." He let out a short, humorless laugh. "Sometimes I thought Tom was crazy, but he lived his faith, I'll say that for him."

"And that was his only asset?" Gawaine asked.

"Of any significance," Richard replied. "He might have a few hundred in his bank account, but no more. He left that to the Trust, too."

"Thank you, I – " Gawaine broke off at the sound of a car engine outside.

Looking through the study window, he saw a taxi draw up outside the garden gate. Inside it, someone was paying the driver.

"Who's next?" Richard asked, with a puzzled look at his sister.

He went out into the hall and opened the outer door, taking a step or two down the path. Susan followed, and Gawaine brought up the rear.

By the time he reached the doorway, the passenger – a young African woman – was getting out of the taxi and pushed the garden gate open, lugging a large suitcase. Gawaine recognised her at once. She was the woman in the photograph from Father Thomas's wallet.

She halted, setting her case down, as Richard and Susan approached down the path. "Who are you?" she demanded. "And where's Tom?"

Chapter Twelve

…graciously hear us, that these evils, which the craft and subtilty of the devil or man worketh against us, be brought to nought.

The Litany

"Oh, you must be Leah!" Susan advanced down the path with her hands held out. "Tom told us so much about you. But…oh, I don't know how to tell you this…"

The young woman – Leah – stared at her. "What?"

"Tom's dead." Susan's voice broke on a sob.

A raw sound of grief came from Leah's throat. A moment later the two women were embracing.

Gawaine, shocked and realizing that he shouldn't be there, ducked back into the vicarage to collect Malcolm Braid's commentary, then fled up the path to the church, with a few murmured words of excuse to Richard.

At the south door he paused, breathing hard, and after a moment let himself inside. Mrs Prestwick had finished her vacuuming, and the church was quiet. Gawaine slipped into the back pew, bowed his head and prayed for the soul of Father Thomas, for Leah, Susan and Richard, for all the pain that stretched its tendrils throughout Ellingwood – and for the one for whom the pain had become intolerable.

Then he gathered up the commentary again and went out, intending to pay a quick visit to the police incident room, and then to look for Malcolm Braid. But as he reached the lychgate, he spotted several people emerging from the back of the church hall across the road, the group breaking up and heading for various cars in the car park.

Among them was Seff Brown. Gawaine drew back into the shadow of the lychgate, hoping she hadn't spotted him, but knowing perfectly well that the hope was vain. He heard the other cars start up and drive away, followed by crisp, determined footsteps crossing the road.

Sighing, Gawaine stepped forward again. "Good morning, Persephone."

Seff gave him a cheerful grin. "Gawaine. What are you – ?" She broke off, her grin fading. "What on earth is the matter? You look as if somebody died."

"Father Thomas died," Gawaine responded.

Seff gazed at him for a moment, then gave a slow nod. "Every time you do this, there's a moment when it hits you. Do you want to talk about it?"

Gawaine knew she was right. It had been a challenge, to consider the possibilities, to discover the grudges against Father Thomas, to examine the terrain on David's map, without too much thought about what lay behind the exercise. Since then his perceptions had shifted. Father Thomas – and his murder – had become real. So had the devastation that his death had caused to the people who loved him.

But he knew also that he couldn't tell Seff why. He would have to mention the people at the vicarage, and Seff would be in duty bound to go down there and interview them. The intrusion was the last thing they needed.

"No, I don't think so," he replied to Seff's question. "But thank you for the offer."

"Where's David?" Seff asked, the question not so much of a *non sequitur* as it might have looked at first.

"At work," Gawaine replied. "He'll be back tonight – he's commuting."

Seff nodded. "Okay. Well, if I can't be your shoulder to cry on, I'd better get on. DCI Ferris just made a statement to the press."

"How obliging…" Gawaine murmured. "Did he say anything interesting?"

"No, just the usual guff. Exploring every avenue… If you ask me, the police are, to coin a phrase, 'baffled.'" She gave Gawaine a beady look, suddenly all efficiency. "Is there anything you can tell me?"

There was quite a lot, Gawaine knew, but nothing that he wanted to see in the following day's headlines. "No new facts have emerged," he said carefully. "Nothing with a bearing on why Father Thomas left the vestry."

Seff narrowed her eyes. "Now there's a weaselly answer if ever I heard one."

"My dear Persephone!"

"All right," Seff said with a sigh. "Have it your own way. But when you can say something, I expect you to say it to me first."

Gawaine nodded reluctantly. He would have much preferred not to say anything at all, but if he had to talk to the press it would be infinitely better to talk to Seff than anyone else.

"Your Mrs Thorpe," he said, realising there was a crumb he could toss her. "Mrs Prestwick. Elderly lady with a vacuum cleaner."

Seff's eyes lit. "Got it!"

Gawaine wished her goodbye and waited until she had crossed the road, got into her car and drove away. Once she was out of sight, he made his way into the incident room at the back of the church hall. To his relief Ferris was not there; a uniformed constable approached him as he entered.

"Can I help you, sir?"

"The churchwardens' staves," Gawaine began. At a look of total incomprehension from the officer, he continued, "Wooden ceremonial rods kept in the church, attached to a couple of pew ends. They have brass tops, about the size and shape of a doorknob."

A light went on in the constable's face. "Right, sir! We'll get them checked."

Duty done, Gawaine bade him goodbye. Then he headed toward the village centre in search of Malcolm Braid.

David's map, becoming a little dog-eared by now, showed Gawaine where the solicitor's office could be found. On the way he passed the doctor's surgery, and remembered what Mrs Prestwick had told him about Louise Braid's pursuit of Dr Jerrold. Gawaine couldn't imagine that Father Thomas, given his track record, would have been happy about that if he had found out about it. He might have admonished her about seeking a relationship with a married man. He might even have refused her Communion, as he had refused it to Ruth Reed.

But then, Gawaine reflected, *the whole village would have known about it.* In any case, he couldn't see Louise Braid as the murderer of Father Thomas. She was too small and slender to have struck those blows. *Unless her brother helped her...*

Gawaine shook his head. The motive was weak in Louise's case, and even weaker in her brother's. Besides, Malcolm Braid had the best of all possible alibis, taking the morning service in front of the whole congregation.

Almost opposite the surgery, Gawaine passed the empty shop which David had mentioned when he gave him the map. Its sign read *Skin Deep* in curly pink letters on a cream ground. *That must have been Chantal's beauty salon.*

Gawaine crossed the road to take a closer look, but the whole of the front of the shop was empty, with nothing remaining of the previous occupant. A TO LET notice was plastered to the window. Continuing, Gawaine tried to convince himself that he was making a fuss about nothing, but he still felt that *l'affaire Chantal* had something important to tell him.

Pushing all that to the back of his mind, Gawaine approached the solicitor's office, a handsome building of ivy-covered brick, bearing a discreet sign that read 'Davenport, Davenport and Braid'. He was in time to spot Malcolm Braid on his way out, and intercepted him at the bottom of the steps.

For a moment the solicitor gave him a puzzled look, as if he didn't remember who Gawaine was. Then his expression cleared. "St Clair – of course. We met at Christabel's. What can I do for you?"

"I came to return this." Gawaine held out the commentary. "Though there are one or two questions I would like to ask you, if you don't mind."

"Feel free." Braid took the commentary and glanced at it before tucking it under his arm. "Thanks – I wondered when I would get that back. Look," he continued, "I was just on my way to the Farrier's Arms for a bite of lunch. Why don't you come with me? We can talk there."

On Gawaine's assent, he led the way back to the centre of the village with long, vigorous strides. Gawaine followed.

The Farrier's Arms stood beside the village green, a thatched, whitewashed building with a mass of dahlias in window boxes; Gawaine winced at the clash of colours. Inside were rustic beams covered with horse brasses, and John Leech hunting prints adorning the walls. The bar was fairly full; Gawaine spotted the Hartleys away in one corner, and was thankful that they didn't seem to have spotted him.

Malcolm Braid slid into a vacant booth as the previous occupants were leaving, and Gawaine took the seat opposite him.

"I can recommend the ploughman's," Braid said, "and they have a very good local bitter here."

Gawaine agreed, quite uninterested in the food, though grateful for a few minutes' grace before he had to start asking questions. Malcolm Braid went to give the order at the bar and returned sooner than Gawaine would have liked with two brimming pints.

"Okay," he said as he took his seat again. "Fire away. Bring on the rack and thumbscrews."

Gawaine couldn't be so light-hearted. "It's good of you to talk to me," he began. "Tell me – when was the last time you saw Father Thomas, before he disappeared?"

"Just the night before," Malcolm told him. "He came to see me, to look over my sermon for the day after. I was down to preach – just as well, as it turned out."

"And he arrived…?"

"About half past seven."

Gawaine felt a tingle of surprise. "You remember that?"

"Oh, yes. Louise had come over for supper, and she was due to babysit the Jerrolds' kids…Dr Jerrold, that she works for. She'd promised to be there at a quarter to eight, so it must have been half seven or just after that she left me. Father Thomas arrived as she was on her way out."

Gawaine blinked. This was all sounding a bit too glib, unless Braid had already been over the facts with DCI Ferris.

"I told all this to the police," Braid said, confirming Gawaine's thought.

"Did Father Thomas stay long?"

"A while." Braid took a long pull at his beer. "I made coffee while Father Thomas read the sermon. We discussed it for a while, and then we got on to discussing the parish."

At that moment Gawaine had to break off his questioning as the barman appeared with two ploughman's lunches. He spent a moment contemplating the food, wondering where the average ploughman would obtain cranberry relish, sliced avocado and pine nuts, then pulled himself together and focused on what he needed to know.

As lay reader, Malcolm Braid must have worked closely with his priest. Gawaine was beginning to realise that he had an ideal opportunity to fill in a little more of the background.

"Was Father Thomas aware that there were problems with the parish?" he asked.

"To some extent. And I have to say, whatever anyone else may have told you, the problems weren't all of Father Thomas's making. St Paul's isn't an easy community."

That seemed aligned with what the bishop had said.

"But you surely didn't approve of what happened to Ruth Reed?" Gawaine ventured cautiously.

"No, but I think Father Thomas was coming to accept that he'd been a bit hasty there. He was mellowing, if you want to put it that way. Don't think of him as a stern moralist calling down hell-fire and damnation on everything he thought was sin. When he found out that I'm divorced, it didn't bother him." Braid paused, neatly cutting off a chunk of Brie. "Of course, I've never remarried."

"So would you have supported his application for the vacancy?" Gawaine asked.

"I think I would." Braid took another pull from his pint. "I think with a bit of help from the bishop he could have been outstanding. I know it's not fashionable to say this…" He shrugged, looking slightly embarrassed. "What I do at St Paul's means a lot to me. When Jim Trask was vicar, it was like pushing a massive rock up a hill."

"Sisyphus," Gawaine murmured.

"Quite. I was really looking forward to working with Father Thomas. It's a pity it's not going to happen."

"He didn't say anything to you that night? Nothing to suggest that there was something bothering him?"

"Something that might have made him decamp the following morning?" Braid shook his head. "Not a thing. We had coffee and a chat, and he left at…oh, maybe about ten. Sailing off on his old rattletrap of a bike, with his cloak billowing out. I never saw him again."

"But DCI Ferris tells me that he sent you a text?"

"That's right. It must have been just a few minutes after he left the vestry, but at that time my phone was switched off, because the service was about to start, and I didn't pick it up until later. I can show you if you want." Braid began fishing in his inside pocket.

"No, that's all right," Gawaine murmured. "But can you tell me what it said?"

Braid frowned thoughtfully. "It was… 'Sorry, I'll explain later. Can you take Evensong?'"

"Then that proves he left the vestry of his own accord," Gawaine said, reflecting that although they had known that already it was good to have it confirmed.

"That's what I can't get my head round," Braid said. "What in the world would make a priest leave his vestry minutes before the service was due to start?"

"None of us can…er… 'get our heads round' it," Gawaine responded. "And until we do, I have the feeling that we'll never know who killed Father Thomas."

Chapter Thirteen

...abate their pride, assuage their malice, and confound their devices.

A Prayer in the time of War and Tumults

David let himself in with the key Gawaine had given him. As he paused in the hall, he could hear the whispery sound of Gawaine's clavichord coming from the music room. He followed the sound and discovered Gawaine intent, unaware of anything around him until he finished the piece in a cascade of notes.

"Festival Hall next week?" David inquired.

Startled, Gawaine looked up. "Oh, the Purcell Room, surely?" he said. "Would you like to hear that piece from the beginning? It's Bach – Carl Philip Emmanuel, of course, not Johann Sebastian."

"No, I would not," David replied, fighting down irritation. Then looking closer he realised that beneath the insouciance Gawaine was looking deeply distressed. "What happened?" he asked.

"I went to the vicarage and met Father Thomas's brother and sister," Gawaine told him. "Richard Coates and Susan Cox. And then this young woman arrived... Leah. I think she must have been Father Thomas's fiancée."

"I didn't think Father Thomas had a family," David said, surprised. "Much less a fiancée."

"Oh, yes. They were…devastated." Gawaine was obviously making a huge effort to control his voice. "You know, David, I've been tackling this all wrong. Father Thomas wasn't some sort of Torquemada intent on whipping his flock into shape. There were people who loved him. The bishop respected him…so did Malcolm Braid, for what that's worth." He sighed. "I suppose I should have learnt by now not to look at anything from Christabel's point of view."

He turned back to the clavichord and began picking out a complicated phrase with one hand.

David had seen his friend retreat like this before, when reality became too overwhelming. He would have had no problem with it, if Gawaine had been able to let the whole thing go. But he never could or would: he had too much conscience, and – though he would have denied it with his last breath – too much courage.

David leant over and firmly closed the lid of the instrument, narrowly avoiding trapping Gawaine's fingers. "Enough of that," he said. "Let's go and find a drink, and see if we can straighten out what we know."

Gawaine hesitated, then gave David a sidelong, guilty look. "All right."

David led the way across the hall to the sitting room and helped himself to a whisky and soda from the drinks table. Gawaine, following, let his hand hover for a moment over the brandy bottle, then splashed a small amount of dry sherry into a glass and went to sit on the couch. The little tortoiseshell cat, curled up asleep on a cushion, woke up and climbed into his lap, miaowing for attention.

Gawaine stroked her absently, visibly relaxing at the sound of her rhythmic purr.

David took a seat by the hearth, evicting the black cat in the process, and earning himself a hiss and a glare from narrowed green eyes.

"So," David said. "Means, motive and opportunity. Who do we have at the top of the list?"

"The person with the best motive still seems to be Frank Reed," Gawaine began, frowning into his glass. David was pleased to see that concentrating on the problem – or the cat – seemed to be pulling him out of his fit of depression. "If he believed that his wife might leave him and take the children with her."

"We don't know that he did believe that," David pointed out.

"No, but for the sake of argument... Motive, then, and means is easy, because anyone can find a blunt instrument and lash out with it. But opportunity..." Gawaine took a meditative sip and set his glass aside. "How did he get Father Thomas out of that vestry?"

David could see the problem. "Father Thomas wouldn't go with him when the service was just about to start. And if Frank Reed had tried to insist, he would have made enough noise that they would have heard it in the church. Which they didn't."

Gawaine reached over for the pad he had been using to make notes on the evening David had arrived. "Right. Frank Reed, possible but unlikely. I suppose I could go and ask him where he was that Sunday morning, but I can't say I like the idea." He gave a theatrical shudder. "He looks frightfully fierce."

"Get DCI Ferris to do it."

"Possible." Gawaine made a note. "Now…John Bretton. Worried about Father Thomas's activities as school chaplain, telling his boys to sell all that they have and give to the poor. Annoyed parents, threatening to withdraw their sons, financial ruin staring Bretton in the face. It's a good motive."

"Not if Bretton could just have told Father Thomas never to darken his door again."

"But could he?" Gawaine scribbled again, looking suddenly more animated. "He seemed to think so, and he was determined that Father Thomas wouldn't get the living, but that could all have been an act for my benefit. Suppose the school chaplaincy was tied to St Paul's… The bishop will know."

David began to feel they might be getting somewhere. "You told me Bretton wasn't in church that Sunday."

"No, he said he was going over some accounts. I wonder if his wife brought him coffee. Or had she gone to church without him?"

"I didn't know he had a wife," David said.

"Mmm. Stella Bretton. And I heard something very interesting about her. I found Seff's Mrs Thorpe this morning, and she told me…"

David listened with growing outrage as Gawaine described his conversation with Mrs Prestwick in the church. "Andrew Danby!" he exploded as Gawaine brought the account to an end. "No wonder he looked so smug when he was telling me about his failed development. He must have known that wasn't really a motive at all. Just pulling the wool over my eyes, and all the while he was sneaking down to the school and – "

"Breaking his marital vows with Mrs Bretton. Yes," said Gawaine.

"Then if Father Thomas had found out," David went on, "Danby would have lost Mrs Danby and Mrs Danby's money. Oh, I'd love to pin it on him!"

"Don't forget he was in church that morning," Gawaine reminded him. "And there's still the problem of how he got Father Thomas to leave the vestry."

"He says he was in church." David was reluctant to abandon his theory, if only because he had disliked Andrew Danby from the moment he set eyes on him. "I'm willing to bet that no one – with the exception of his wife – would be sure enough of that to swear to it in court. And Marjorie isn't likely to shop him, is she?"

"Not if she didn't know about Stella Bretton," Gawaine responded, busily making notes. "You may be onto something there, my dear David."

"And then there's Colonel Sutton," David continued, shelving for the moment the desirable vision of DCI Ferris dragging Andrew Danby off to jail. "Mentally undressing the Young Wives. At least it wasn't the choirboys," he added.

"Please..." Gawaine shuddered. "Besides, Mrs Prestwick didn't think he'd done any more than look," he reminded David.

David thought that Gawaine was far too inclined to believe the best of people – at least for someone trying to track down a murderer. "But we don't know that," he said. "Suppose some outraged Young Wife had gone to Father Thomas...?" When Gawaine did not respond, he added, "Do you think you ought to question them?"

"Heaven forbid," Gawaine replied. "At least, not for the moment. *That* would really put the cat among the pigeons. I'm supposed to be averting scandal, not fomenting it."

David saw his point. "Okay, then, what about the Hartleys? Either of them, or both together. Did the bishop get back to you about the church accounts?"

Gawaine shook his head. "I suppose it takes longer than a day or two to get the audit done. But they were supposedly jetlagged after their flight, and their only alibi is each other."

"Frank Reed, John Bretton, Colonel Sutton, Andrew Danby and the Hartleys." David ticked each of their suspects off on his fingers. "All of them threatened in some way by Father Thomas's extreme views."

"If you call objecting to adultery or embezzlement an extreme view," Gawaine said. "Besides, Malcolm Braid told me that Father Thomas was mellowing. He'd come to accept that he'd made a mistake over Ruth Reed."

David shrugged. "Whatever. The point I'm trying to make is, are we restricting ourselves? We're tending to look for people with guilty secrets – and there are enough of those, considering Ellingwood is a typical English village."

"My dear David!" Gawaine looked shocked. "The typical English village is a hotbed of illicit passion."

"Are you speaking from experience?" David asked, stifling laughter. He couldn't think of anyone less likely than Gawaine to indulge in illicit passion.

Gawaine examined exquisitely manicured fingernails. "Certainly not. But when people are thrown together, things like this...rise to the surface, like dead bodies."

"Yes, and to get back to our own personal dead body, shouldn't we be looking for other possible motives? For example, I don't suppose you managed to find out anything about Father Thomas's will?"

"I did, but there's nothing relevant in it," Gawaine replied. "He divided his shares between his brother and sister, but all the income was to go to the Nazareth Trust – the group that he was working with in Africa. So no one but the Trust gained anything."

"I'm not so sure about that," David said, a suspicion creeping its way into his mind. "You don't happen to know how many shares the three of them owned? I mean, the proportions?"

Gawaine looked puzzled. "I do, as it happens…if you think it matters. Richard Coates owned forty per cent, and Thomas and Susan thirty per cent each."

"And Thomas divided his shares equally?"

Gawaine nodded, still looking puzzled. "But I told you, they don't get any extra money."

David looked at him. He had long suspected that Gawaine wasn't as unworldly as he pretended: indeed, that the pretence was no more than a way of winding him up. Usually he found it an engaging quirk. But on this occasion he realised that Gawaine really had no idea of what the will meant.

"Honestly," he said with a sigh of exasperation. "How someone as intelligent as you can be so obtuse and still have a pulse, I'll never understand. It's not about money, Gawaine, it's about control. Look."

He crossed the room, grabbed the pad from Gawaine's hands and ripped off the top sheet, now covered with

Gawaine's meticulous handwriting. "Here's the starting point. Richard has forty per cent, Thomas and Susan have thirty." He drew three circles and labelled them. "No one person has control. Any two of them can outvote the third. Then Thomas dies. Now Richard has fifty-five per cent, and Susan has forty-five." He split Thomas's circle down the middle and drew arrows to show the division of his shares. "Therefore, Richard controls the company."

Gawaine studied the diagram, then looked up at David, blue eyes bemused. "Fascinating."

David shook his head. "You still don't get it, do you? If there are any arguments about the way the company is run, Richard wins. Susan can't outvote him. I'd say that was a pretty good motive, myself."

"But…Richard and Susan weren't quarrelling. They were grieving for Father Thomas."

David shrugged. "Just because they weren't clawing each other's eyes out doesn't mean there weren't clashes in the boardroom." He looked down at Gawaine. "I know. You liked them, didn't you?"

Gawaine nodded mutely, looking distressed again. David briefly wished that he hadn't let himself be carried away by his theory, then pushed the thought away. It wasn't the first time Gawaine had been emotionally involved with a murderer, and he guessed it wouldn't be the last. He wouldn't have respected Gawaine half as much as he did, if his friend had been able to detach himself and look at the affair as no more than a puzzle.

"And I can tell you how he could have got Father Thomas out of the vestry," David went on.

Gawaine glanced up. "How?"

"Richard drives up to the vicarage, doesn't see his brother there, comes up to the church by the footpath. Opens the vestry door. 'Thomas, there's been an accident. Susan's dying. You've got to come.' Easy."

Gawaine thought for a moment, then nodded reluctantly. "You could be right."

"Then Thomas sends the text, Richard drives him off, and in a quiet spot bops him and dumps the body." When Gawaine didn't respond, he added, "I think you should ask DCI Ferris to find out if Richard Coates has an alibi for that Sunday morning."

Chapter Fourteen

...the mutual help and comfort each shall have of the other.

The Solemnisation of Matrimony

Next morning Gawaine had barely finished showering and dressing when he heard the doorbell ring. Hurrying downstairs, he saw Mrs Summers opening the front door, and realised with alarm that his visitors were Susan Cox and the African woman, Leah. He greeted them with some trepidation, wishing that David had not already departed for London.

"We're sorry to bother you," Susan said. "But there's something we want to ask you, if you don't mind."

"Of course not. Come in."

Gawaine almost ushered the two women into the sitting room, until he remembered that his notes from the night before were still lying around, along with David's diagram of the distribution of the shares. Instead, he led them through into the conservatory, asking Mrs Summers to bring coffee.

"This is lovely!" Susan exclaimed as she stepped inside the room, gazing around at the green banks of fern, the delicate sprays of orchids and the over-arching cascade of white bougainvillaea.

"I have bougainvillaea in my garden at home," Leah said. "The white is the rarest kind, and the most beautiful, I think."

"This is Leah Koroma," Susan said as Gawaine drew up chairs. "She and Tom were going to be married."

"I guessed as much," Gawaine responded, feeling a pang of pain at the grief in Leah's dark eyes. "I'm so sorry."

"I still can't believe it," Leah said. "It was such a shock…"

She was a beautiful woman, tall and slim, her hair plaited in cornrows with a bright bead on the end of each plait. With the chance to study her more closely, Gawaine realised that she was one of the people in the photograph he had seen in the vestry.

"You hadn't heard that Father Thomas had disappeared?" he asked.

Leah shook her head. "I'm one of the local workers for the Nazareth Trust," she explained. "I was living up country to help with the latest project. There's no phone or internet up there. The last I heard was a letter from Tom, inviting me to come over. Even that had taken a long time to reach me." Her voice shook. "If it had been quicker, maybe…"

"Were you coming here to get married?" Gawaine asked, shivering inwardly at the thought of how Leah's life had changed without warning.

"No, not this time," Leah replied. "Tom didn't want us to marry until he had a job. He told me he was applying to work here, and he wanted me to see if I'd like living in Ellingwood." She managed to smile. "This is so different from home, but I would have lived anywhere with Tom."

Gawaine was relieved that Mrs Summers appeared at that moment with the coffee tray. When he had poured, and everyone was settled, he asked, "What is it I can do for you?"

"We wondered if you knew anything about Tom's cross," Susan said.

"His cross?"

"When Tom and I got engaged, he gave me this ring." Leah stretched out her hand to show Gawaine a ring made of polished ebony, the upper surface flat and inlaid with a cross in silver. "I gave him a cross made by the same craftsman. He always wore it, but now we can't find it anywhere."

"We practically took the vicarage apart looking for it," Susan continued. "We even tried the garage and the saddlebag of Tom's bike, though goodness knows why he would have put the cross in there. Then we went to see the police, and they told us it hadn't been found on his body."

"Did you try the vestry?" Gawaine asked, hoping that Susan didn't think he might have filched the cross while he was searching the vicarage.

Susan nodded. "We tracked down one of the churchwardens... Mrs Cottesmore. She phoned the sacristan to come over and let us in. She wasn't too pleased with you," she added to Gawaine. "She said you'd borrowed her keys and not returned them."

Gawaine winced. In the stress of the day before, he had completely forgotten that he was carrying Christabel's set of church keys.

"I'll go over later and apologise," he said, wondering if flowers would be sufficient propitiation, or whether Christabel would demand blood. "So you searched the vestry but you didn't find the cross there?"

"No," said Susan. "The sacristan was really helpful. He let us check both vestries, and he even opened the safe for us in case it had been put away for safe keeping, but it wasn't there. We wondered if you might have seen it, or if you could think of somewhere else we might look."

Gawaine took a thoughtful sip of coffee. "You're sure he had it here? He didn't accidentally leave it behind in Africa, or lose it on the journey? Or could he have left it where he first stayed when he came back to this country?"

Leah shook her head, her beads glittering. "He cared more about it than that."

"He stayed with Richard and his wife when he first came home," Susan said, "He had it then, and later he definitely had it here. Richard and I came to stay for a week-end shortly after he moved to Ellingwood, and he was wearing it then."

Curiouser and curiouser, Gawaine thought. "Then I don't know where it might be," he said. "But I think it might be important to track it down."

Susan gave a firm nod of agreement. "Leah would like to have it."

"Not only that," Gawaine said. "But if Father Thomas always wore it, then he must have been wearing it when he left the vestry, the morning when he was last seen. As it wasn't with his body, it's likely that the murderer took it."

Leah let out a gasp and pressed one hand to her lips.

"Why?" Susan asked. "It wasn't valuable – not in that way. Not worth stealing."

"A good question," Gawaine murmured. "What did it look like? No – wait a moment."

125

He rose and went into the sitting-room to fetch his note pad and a pencil, making sure that the evidence of his discussion with David was left safely behind. Another thought struck him while he was on his way back, and he paused by the telephone and looked up the number of Davenport, Davenport and Braid. A moment later he was speaking to Malcolm Braid.

"When Father Thomas visited you on the night before he disappeared," Gawaine asked, "was he wearing his pectoral cross?"

"That African thing?" Braid paused, then continued thoughtfully, "Do you know, I don't really remember. I assume he was, but I couldn't in all honesty swear to it. Why – is it important?"

"It might be," Gawaine replied. "It's gone missing. If you happen to come across it, could you let me know?"

"Of course," Braid said, and rang off.

Dissatisfied – for he had hoped to pinpoint more accurately when the cross had disappeared – Gawaine continued to the conservatory.

"I'm sorry to keep you waiting," he said. "I hoped Malcolm Braid might be able to help us." He explained about the phone call, then sat down again with the pad on his lap. "Now," he continued. "Describe the cross to me, and I'll draw it."

Leah leant closer to him so that she could see the pad. "It was about four or five inches high," she began. "Each arm of the cross bulged out a bit, then tapered to the end – no, more elongated than that. The silver part was exactly the same, but finer..."

After a few false starts, and giving Leah the pencil so

she could show him what she meant, Gawaine managed to produce a satisfactory drawing of the missing cross.

"It hung from a leather thong," Susan said. "I suppose the thong might have broken, but Tom would surely have noticed." Turning to Leah, she added, "That's an idea. It might have broken in the vicarage garden, when…" Her voice trailed off.

"When they took him away," Leah said, her gaze clouded, imagining.

"It's worth checking," Susan said briskly, rising to her feet. "Come on. Thank you for your help, Mr St Clair."

Gawaine rose with the two women. "I haven't done very much," he responded. "But I'll try to think where the cross might be. Let me know if you find it. And can you give me a telephone number where I can reach you?"

Susan delved into her bag and produced the business card of a hotel in Guildford.

When Gawaine had ushered the two women out, he returned to the conservatory and studied the picture of the cross. He already had a good idea of what might have happened to it.

"If the murderer took it," he murmured aloud, addressing the bougainvillaea above his head, "then it's probably at the bottom of the nearest river, along with the mobile phone."

He wondered what use he could make of his drawing. If he shoved it under the nose of his suspects and asked, "Have you seen this?" would he get a reaction? Or would they simply reply, "Yes, it's Father Thomas's cross," and he would be no further forward. Or even worse, he might warn the murderer that he was getting close to solving the mystery.

"If only that were true," he sighed.

Determined to make progress somehow, Gawaine drove over to Ellingwood and parked once again in the church car park. Taking the drawing with him, he walked around the back of the hall to beard DCI Ferris in his den.

The room had even more detritus of plastic cups and biscuit wrappers, and the whiteboard at the far end had acquired more notes and photographs. But DCI Ferris still had the same irritable expression.

"Now what?" he growled, shoving a file at one of his subordinates and turning to Gawaine.

"Good morning, Chief Inspector," Gawaine began, clinging to civilized discourse even in the midst of hostility. He held out the drawing. "I thought you might be interested in seeing this."

Ferris gave it a cursory glance. "And this is?"

"Father Thomas's cross. I believe his sister asked you about it. He always wore it, but it wasn't with his body."

A flicker of interest appeared for a moment on Ferris's face. "I suppose it might be useful," he admitted grudgingly. He took the drawing and waved it at a passing uniformed constable. "Take a photocopy of that. It looks as though the murderer must have taken the cross," he continued to Gawaine. "God knows why."

Gawaine reflected that He certainly did.

"Could be to delay identification, along with the phone," Ferris went on. "I doubt he would hang on to it, though, and in any case I can't ask for a warrant to search the premises of every possible suspect to see if they're hiding it somewhere."

Gawaine still felt that it was illogical for the murderer to have taken the cross and the phone, while leaving

Father Thomas still dressed in his cassock and clerical collar, if his only reason was to hide the priest's identity. But Ferris seemed satisfied to believe that, and Gawaine had no intention of starting an argument with him.

"You have possible suspects?" he asked delicately, not sure if he would get an answer.

"Your bishop clued me in on the Church Treasurer," Ferris replied. "The audit is under way. And Richard Coates…he gets control of his company now that his brother's dead."

Gawaine made an intelligent murmur, grateful for David's lesson in the workings of high finance. "Do you know where he was that Sunday morning?"

"I'm going to bring him in for questioning," Ferris replied. "If he can't establish a solid alibi, he's in big trouble."

Worriedly Gawaine realised that DCI Ferris was taking Richard Coates seriously as his brother's murderer. Perhaps he too had come to the same conclusions as David about the way Richard could have persuaded Father Thomas to leave the vestry.

"By the way," Ferris went on, "thanks for the tip about the churchwardens' rods. I sent them over to forensics. Mind you, if Richard Coates is our man, it's unlikely he would have used one."

Gawaine murmured agreement, hoping that the examination would find something. It would be useful evidence in Richard's favour.

The constable returned with the original drawing, handed it to Gawaine and went to stick the photocopy to the whiteboard. Gawaine gracefully took his leave, unwilling to share any of his other suspicions.

"Please let me know if you find the cross," he said.

Ferris replied only with a grunt; Gawaine optimistically tried to assume that it conveyed assent.

Returning to his car, he headed for the Reeds' garden centre, hoping that a gift of flowers might mollify Christabel for the inconvenience of being without her church keys. When he arrived, there was no sign of Ruth Reed or the children, but he spotted Frank Reed potting out plants in one of the greenhouses.

Gawaine hesitated, wondering whether to tackle him about his alibi, or lack of it, for the Sunday morning when Father Thomas had disappeared. Frank Reed was a large man, and when Gawaine and David had met him briefly on their previous visit, he had not looked friendly. Still, Gawaine reflected, Reed was unlikely to assault him in full view of the garden centre customers.

While he was dithering, Frank Reed evidently noticed that he was there, and waved him over. Gawaine entered the greenhouse cautiously.

"Wallflowers," he said brightly, hoping to establish a friendly rapport.

Reed nodded. "We sell a lot of these, this time of year, for early spring flowering." He thrust another tiny plant into its appropriate pot, then added, "Ruth tells me you're looking into this murder for the bishop."

"That's right."

Frank Reed let out a snort. "I'm surprised you haven't come to see me before this. Aren't I your number one suspect?"

Gawaine blinked. That was the last thing he had expected Reed to say, and in a tone that was half humorous.

"Come on," Frank Reed said when after a few seconds Gawaine had not replied. "That idiot at St Paul's wanted to take my wife and kids away from me. I tell you straight, I'd have thumped him with pleasure."

"And did you?" Gawaine asked.

"No, I did not. I don't go in for religion and vicars telling me what to do, but I wouldn't have killed him. A black eye now, just to tell him to keep his nose out of my business... But I didn't even do that. I knew it would upset Ruth, and I knew she wasn't going anywhere, so..." He shrugged.

Gawaine was inclined to believe him; he liked his straightforward manner. But he had met several plausible murderers in his time.

"So where were you that Sunday morning?" he asked.

Frank Reed didn't reply for a moment, his strong, blunt fingers pressing each seedling into the dark compost. "I was here," he said at last. "Getting everything ready. We open at ten on Sundays."

Gawaine realised that an opening time of ten didn't mean that Frank Reed couldn't have been murdering Father Thomas at nine fifteen. "I know Mrs Reed and the children were on their way to St John's," he said. "Is there anyone else who can confirm you were here?"

"Yes, I have a couple of teenagers who help me at the weekend," Frank Reed replied readily. "I can give you their phone numbers if you want."

"No, not at present, thank you," Gawaine responded. "I'll ask you if I need them."

He couldn't help thinking that Reed was being a bit too co-operative. *He might be trying to pull the wool over*

131

my eyes, just as Andrew Danby did with David. It also occurred to him that perhaps Reed had hit Father Thomas, just a bit too hard. The priest could have fallen and struck his head… It might not be murder at all, he thought hopefully, then discarded the theory, remembering that two blows had been struck to kill Father Thomas.

"Then is that all?" Frank Reed asked. He had finished the seedlings, and began to load the pots onto a flat wooden tray.

"For now," Gawaine murmured. "I'm grateful to you for being so helpful."

Frank Reed narrowed his eyes. "And maybe you're thinking I'm being a bit too helpful?"

Gawaine said nothing, taken aback that Reed had followed his thoughts so accurately.

"I'll tell you why," Reed went on. "Sales have fallen off since the murder, and I've spotted a few of my customers looking at me funny. I'll be glad when my name's cleared."

"I'm sure you will," Gawaine agreed. "In fact I'm sure there are plenty of people in Ellingwood who'll be glad when this is all over."

"Except the murderer," Frank Reed said heavily.

Gawaine nodded. "Except the murderer."

And maybe even the murderer, he thought as he took his leave. *The guilt, and the secrecy…that must be a terrible burden to bear.*

Gawaine bought a bunch of shaggy bronze chrysanthemums in the garden centre shop, and presented himself at Christabel's mock Tudor residence.

"About time," Christabel said as she let him in. She gave the flowers a suspicious look, as if she was scanning them for earwigs. "I don't suppose it occurs to you, Gawaine, that it's very inconvenient to be left without the keys."

"I know, I'm sorry," Gawaine replied. He entered the house as Christabel stepped back ungraciously to let him in.

Christabel took the flowers and headed for the kitchen to find a vase. Gawaine followed, fishing the set of keys out of his pocket. He set them down on the worktop and glanced around, somewhat intimidated by the gleam of stainless steel and assorted gadgetry.

"Would you like coffee?" Christabel asked, raising her voice over the sound of the running tap.

Gawaine felt something of the apprehension that a medieval Roman might have experienced on being offered wine by the Borgias. "No, thank you. I have to be getting on."

"I should think so too." Christabel placed the flowers in the vase and twitched them skilfully into an attractive arrangement. "You don't seem to have made much progress so far."

"It's early days," Gawaine murmured. He had no intention of sharing any of his speculations with Christabel. "Less than a week since the body was found."

Christabel snorted, but made no comment in words. "I assume you had a visit from Susan Cox and that African woman," she continued. "I don't suppose you know anything about this missing cross."

"No, but we made a drawing of it," Gawaine replied, sliding it out from his pocket. "Is that how you remember it?"

Christabel glanced at the sheet of paper. "Something like it. I didn't really take much notice of it."

"Was Father Thomas wearing it when you last saw him?" Gawaine asked, still clinging to the theory that the priest might have lost the cross quite innocently, before he was killed.

Christabel frowned. "Let me think. The last time I saw him…that was on the Saturday, the night before he disappeared. Charles and I saw him cycling through the village. But it was a nasty night, and he was wearing his cloak, so I couldn't see whether he had the cross on or not. Does this really matter?"

"It might," said Gawaine.

Christabel gave him a look that was all too familiar: a suggestion that his mind, never too stable to begin with, had fragmented completely. "Before that…" she began with a sigh. "Before that was the previous Sunday's service. He was wearing the cross then."

"Thank you." So unless Father Thomas had lost the cross in the week before he died, his murderer must have taken it. "Tell me – Mrs Cox checked the vicarage and the vestry. Is there anywhere else Father Thomas might have left the cross?"

Christabel shrugged. "No. Unless he left it lying around in the church. He used to hide little crucifixes under the altar cloths. Just another of these High Church practices… so unsuitable."

Gawaine thought that Father Thomas would hardly have left this cross lying around – not the precious cross that Leah had given him. But he supposed it would be worth checking.

"I'll go and look now," he said, grateful for the excuse of getting out alive and relatively unmauled. "Thank you."

"Well, I hope you manage to make sense of all this soon," Christabel said as she ushered him to the door. "I'm thinking of calling an extraordinary meeting of the PCC. You can give us your report then."

Gawaine shuddered and fled.

Chapter Fifteen

Grant us grace to forsake all covetous desires and
inordinate love of riches.

The Collect for St Matthew's Day

Gawaine left Christabel's house and walked down to the
church, mulling over the problem of Father Thomas's
pectoral cross. Though commonsense told him that the
murderer must have taken the cross and either dumped
it or destroyed it, he couldn't shake off the feeling that
somehow its whereabouts must be significant.

When he let himself into the church, Gawaine heard
the sound of movement coming from the side chapel. A
moment later Beryl Hartley appeared, carrying a small
watering can.

"Oh, it's you," she said. "Can I help you?" She flourished
the can. "I was just freshening up the flowers."

Gawaine walked up the side aisle to meet her. She
didn't sound hostile, but he couldn't imagine that she
would be pleased to see him. Her next words didn't inspire
him with confidence.

"You know my husband is gunning for you?"

"Oh, really?" Gawaine said faintly, aware that the whole
of Ellingwood might be gunning for him if he wasn't very
careful. "How perfectly frightful."

"He wasn't pleased when the bishop called for an audit of the church accounts. He thinks you're responsible."

Gawaine took a deep breath. "I am," he said. "I suggested it to the bishop."

To his surprise, Beryl Hartley was eyeing him tolerantly. "After what that little cat Louise said about us not being able to afford our holiday, I suppose. If I were you, I shouldn't pay much attention to what she says."

"She spreads gossip?" Gawaine asked.

"Not really. She just likes to get little digs in wherever she can." Beryl hesitated, then went on. "I shouldn't be nasty about her, but sometimes she is the limit! No one would have anything to do with her if it wasn't for her brother. Malcolm is a decent sort, so we all put up with Louise for his sake."

Gawaine nodded, discovering a hitherto untapped well of sympathy for Louise Braid. Did she know she was only tolerated because of Malcolm? She couldn't be a very happy person. Perhaps the 'little digs' were her only form of defence.

"And are they accurate, these remarks she makes?" he asked.

Beryl stared at him as if the question shocked her. "You've got a nerve!' she said. "Are you really expecting me to tell you whether Henry paid for our cruise with money from church funds?"

Gawaine eased a pace backwards, eyeing the watering can warily. It had a long, pointed spout which looked capable of a lot of damage. "It would be very helpful if you could…er…clear that up."

To his surprise, Beryl let out a chuckle, genuinely warm and humorous. "I promise you, he didn't," she replied.

She crossed in front of the altar and poked the watering can spout into the pedestal arrangement beneath the pulpit. Gawaine took a moment to appreciate the flowers, a blaze of scarlet and orange dahlias, lighting up the church.

Beryl Hartley turned back to him when she had finished her watering. "I suppose I'd better tell you the truth," she said. "But can you promise me it won't go any further?"

"If it's not relevant to Father Thomas's murder," Gawaine responded.

"It's not. It's not even anything awful, just embarrassing." Her tanned, rather leathery complexion was actually reddening. "I won the money on a horse."

Gawaine blinked in bewilderment. "Then why – ?" he began.

"Why is it such a deadly secret? That's because of Henry. He's rabidly anti-gambling, and the whole church knows it. It's as much as anyone can do to get him to buy a raffle ticket. So if it ever came out that I'd placed a bet at a race track…" She shook her head, half amused, half helpless.

"So why did you?"

"We have friends who own a half share in a racehorse," Beryl explained. "It was running at a race meeting at Epsom, and they invited us to go with them to watch. Henry wouldn't set foot on a race track, of course, but I thought it would be fun, so I went. I never intended to bet, but when I got there my friends put me under a lot of pressure to 'have a little flutter'. So I did. Their beast was a rank outsider, and I thought it would have no chance of winning, so Henry need never know about it."

"But it did win?"

"The wretched creature streaked past the post way ahead of the rest of the field. And I won an indecent amount of money. There was no way of hiding that from Henry."

"I imagine he wasn't pleased?" Gawaine murmured.

"He was furious. At first he wanted me to give the lot to charity, and we did discuss it, but we really needed a holiday. We'd been working hard – voluntary work, we're both retired – and having the extension built had been very stressful. So we put half of my winnings towards the cruise, and gave the other half to Save the Children."

"I understand." Gawaine was beginning to make sense now of the whole affair. "It would be awkward for your husband if the truth got out."

"He would be devastated. He would be the laughing-stock of the whole congregation, because he has such rigid principles about gambling. But we thought it would be fairly safe, because the friends I was with aren't local, and they don't know anyone else here."

"And what if Father Thomas had found out?" Gawaine asked.

"I might have had my knuckles rapped, I suppose," Beryl replied. "But – oh, now I see. You think Henry might have killed Father Thomas to keep his guilty secret. Well, you're wrong. Father Thomas didn't know, and even if he had found out, he wasn't the sort of person to spread it around. Besides, Henry was with me that morning."

Gawaine didn't point out that Beryl would not be the first wife to give her husband a false alibi. She might, like Andrew Danby, have tried to fob him off with a weak motive to cover up something far more serious.

"You won't tell anyone else?" Beryl asked anxiously.

Gawaine shook his head. "As I said, not unless it becomes relevant, and it's unlikely that it will."

Beryl visibly relaxed. "So is there anything else I can help you with?" she asked. "Were you looking for someone?"

"For something, actually." Gawaine slid the drawing of the cross out of his pocket. "I suppose you recognize this."

Beryl glanced at the drawing. "Yes, it's Father Thomas's cross." She gave Gawaine a puzzled look. "Why are you showing me?"

"Because the cross is missing," Gawaine explained. "It wasn't with Father Thomas when he was found, and it's not in the vicarage or the vestry. I wondered if it might be somewhere here in the church."

"Odd. I shouldn't imagine he would leave something like that lying about," Beryl said. She waved a hand around the church. "Feel free to look. I'll help if you like."

"Thank you."

Beryl deposited her watering can on the pulpit steps and went to the back of the church to check the shelves where the service books were kept, leaving Gawaine to search in the sanctuary and the side chapel – the Lady Chapel, he realised, from the rendition of the Annunciation in the stained glass window: the Angel Gabriel in a glory of wings, holding out a lily to Mary, who gazed at him awestruck. Gawaine discovered the crucifixes Christabel had mentioned, concealed beneath the altar covers, but no sign of the cross he was looking for.

"There's nothing at the back," Beryl reported, joining him in the chapel. "And if it had been dropped on the floor somehow, Mrs Prestwick or one of the others on the cleaning team would have found it."

Gawaine made a final foray into the pulpit, nervously negotiating the rickety steps, but the cross wasn't there either. He had to admit defeat, becoming more and more convinced that the murderer must have been responsible for the cross's disappearance.

He thanked Beryl and left the church. As he walked down the path to the lychgate he wondered what he ought to do next. Everything he had tried was coming to a dead end. Henry Hartley, one of his most promising suspects, seemed to be in the clear, if his wife was telling the truth. Frank Reed, too, was looking less likely.

"I really ought to get out of this habit of *believing* people," Gawaine murmured to himself.

Still not seeing any way forward, he walked towards Christabel's house, where he had left his car. Before he was halfway there, a cheerful voice behind him said, "Hi!"

Gawaine winced and turned to see Seff Brown smiling at him. She was stylishly dressed as always in a turquoise jacket with a long, lime-green silk scarf.

"Surely you've got something for me this time?" she asked.

Gawaine was about to deny any such thing when a thought struck him. "I may indeed," he said, once again fishing out the drawing of the cross.

"Nice," she said, examining it. "Now tell me why I should be interested."

Gawaine launched into the story of how Leah Koroma, Father Thomas's fiancée, had given him the cross, and how it was now missing. As he explained, the look of a cat that has filched the cream spread over Seff's face.

"Oh, I can run with this," she said. "I don't suppose you can tell me where to find this...Leah?"

"You suppose correctly, my dear Persephone," Gawaine replied, perfectly aware that he would not have told Seff even if he had known where Leah was staying.

"Oh, well." Seff shrugged. "I'll track her down. Meanwhile, is it okay if I keep the drawing? We can print it in the paper. 'Have You Seen This Cross?' It might even turn up some sort of clue to the murderer."

"It might," Gawaine conceded, glancing warily around for flying pigs. "You can take it and have it copied, but I'll need it back. And it might be as well to let DCI Ferris know what you're planning, before you print anything."

"Hmm... You could be right." Seff slid the drawing into her bag and turned away in the direction of the church hall and the incident room. A moment later she turned back. "Why don't you come and have dinner with me tonight?" she asked. "David too, of course. Then I can give you back the drawing."

"Thank you." Gawaine felt slightly nervous at the thought of a whole evening with Seff, but it would have been boorish to refuse.

"Great! The Farrier's Arms, half past seven, okay? I'm staying there."

"I thought you wanted to stay with me," Gawaine said, privately admitting to a certain relief.

Seff grinned. "I wouldn't dream of sullying your reputation. Besides I need to be in the middle of things.

Half seven, then. I'll see you there." With a cheery wave, she was gone.

Gawaine wandered off to find his car, asking himself whether he, like Seff, should be living in the middle of things, and guiltily grateful that he wasn't.

He stopped off for a late lunch on his way home, and the afternoon was well advanced by the time he turned into his drive. To his surprise, he saw Leah Koroma hunched up on his doorstep, her head in her hands and her suitcase by her side. As he stopped the car and got out, she sprang up and rushed towards him.

"You have to help me!" she exclaimed.

"Yes, of course, if I can," Gawaine said immediately. "What happened?"

"The police have arrested Richard for murdering his brother."

For a few seconds Gawaine stared at her, surprised by how quickly DCI Ferris was working. Then he realised that Richard was probably just being questioned; the formal arrest would come later, if he couldn't give a good account of himself. But the distinction would be unimportant to Leah.

"They came to the hotel this morning," Leah went on. "They took Richard, and his car, too. And Susan went with them. So I couldn't stay there any longer, not if there's any chance they killed Tom."

Her tears spilled over, and she wiped at them with the palm of her hand.

"Come inside," Gawaine said, touching her on the shoulder and leading her towards the house. "I'm sorry

143

you've had to wait out here, but my housekeeper leaves at mid-day."

He let Leah in, and carried her suitcase into the hall. She stood still, glancing around in confusion.

"Maybe I shouldn't have come," she said. "But since Tom died, I don't know anyone in this country except for Richard and Susan."

"You did exactly the right thing," Gawaine said. "You can tell me all about it. But first…have you eaten? Would you like something?"

Leah shook her head, still trying to control her tears. "It doesn't matter…"

Without another word, Gawaine led her into the kitchen and sat her at the table while he plated a portion of the cold chicken and salad Mrs Summers had left in the fridge, and a glass of apple juice.

"You know," he said diffidently as he set up the coffee percolator, "just because the police are questioning Richard doesn't mean that he did it. There could be any number of other explanations."

Leah raised tragic eyes towards him. "But he gained from Tom's death."

"So did plenty of other people." Realising that comment was not particularly helpful, Gawaine added, "The police will need hard evidence before they arrest him. This could all be over in a few hours."

He watched Leah as she ate in silence for a few moments, then shook her head slowly. "Richard and Susan were so kind," she said at last. "I thought I could trust them, but now…I don't want to see them again. I just want to go home." Something flashed in her eyes, and she added, "But I'm not going anywhere until I find out what happened to Tom."

"No, of course not," Gawaine murmured.

"But then what am I to do?" Leah said. "I can't go back to that hotel – I *can't* – but I don't have anywhere else I can go."

"You can stay here," Gawaine offered immediately.

Leah looked up, startled and suddenly embarrassed. Gawaine realised that she might have a problem with staying alone under the same roof as a single man. He thought of reassuring her that he was harmless, then reflected that she had no reason to believe him. And he dared not even mention David's presence.

"No, that's a bad idea," he said. "I have a better one. Finish your meal while I make a phone call."

Going out into the hall and closing the kitchen door behind him, Gawaine dialled the number of the Farrier's Arms and to his relief was put through straight away to Seff.

"I have Leah Koroma here," he told her.

"Leah!" Seff exclaimed. "Gawaine, that's brilliant! I tracked her to the hotel in Guildford where she was staying with Richard Coates and his sister, but they all seem to have flown the coop. Can I come over and talk to her?"

Rapidly Gawaine explained to her what had happened, aware of excitement rippling off Seff in waves and down the telephone wires into his ear.

"This is going to be such a scoop!" she said when he had finished.

"I'm not telling you for a scoop," Gawaine responded. "Leah's upset – and who can wonder – and she needs someone to look after her. Can you get her a room at the Farrier's Arms?"

"Hang on," Seff said. "I'll check." A moment later she returned and added, "Yes, there's a room vacant. Can you bring her over?"

Her excitement had vanished, replaced – as Gawaine had hoped – by an air of practical good sense.

"Yes, I'll bring her," he replied. "And, my dear Persephone, I trust you to go easy on her. If she doesn't want to talk to you, then don't…what's the word David used? Don't 'bug' her."

"I promise, she shall be unbugged," Seff said. "But I won't say the same for Richard Coates, if I can get at him. This case could be about to break."

"I doubt it," Gawaine said, but Seff had already put the phone down.

Chapter Sixteen

From fornication, and all other deadly sin; and from all
the deceits of the world, the flesh and the devil, Good Lord
deliver us.

The Litany

"Busy day," David commented as he put his car into
gear and set off towards Ellingwood.

Gawaine had just finished describing his various
encounters, including the whole business of the cross,
which David tended to dismiss as a red herring. It was
obvious to him that the murderer had taken it in the
hope of delaying identification of the body, and by now
it would be buried, burnt, or dropped into a convenient
river.

"So what happens now?" he asked.

Gawaine's only reply was an unintelligible murmur.
David thought he was looking strung-out, as if it was all
getting on top of him.

Nothing new there, David thought. *But there's no point
telling him to leave it to the police. Not now he's got a damsel
in distress.*

"I shall try to see DCI Ferris about Richard Coates,"
Gawaine said, rousing himself after a moment. "I find it
hard to believe he's guilty."

"You never want to believe anyone's guilty," David pointed out. "But if Ferris nails him, you can give up worrying, the Ellingwood lot can stop giving each other the evil eye, and Leah can go home. Win-win."

"Except for Richard Coates," Gawaine responded. "Especially if he didn't do it."

David gave up. "Whatever."

As they approached the church on the way to the Farrier's Arms, David spotted several cars parked in the hall car park, and a number of people standing around, chatting in small groups.

"David!" Gawaine said suddenly. "Turn in. I've had an idea."

With little warning, David rammed a foot down on the brake and turned into the entrance with a stylish skid. "What idea?" he asked as he drew the car to a halt. "We're going to be late at the pub."

"I've seen someone I want to talk to. It won't take long."

He got out of the car, and David followed. Lights were on in the church hall, casting yellow oblongs onto the surface of the car park. The sound of a piano, energetically thumped, drifted into the air.

Gawaine approached the nearest group, spoke to one of the women there, and drew her a little way from the others. She was plump and dark-haired, dressed in jeans and a scarlet sweatshirt, and she looked rather reluctant, casting an anxious glance back at her friends as she moved away with Gawaine.

"I don't have much time," she was saying as David joined them. "I'm here to pick Katie up from her ballet class, and I don't want her bothered."

"I'll be as quick as I can," Gawaine promised. Turning to David, he added, "This is David Powers, who's helping me with this...affair. David, this is Jennifer Rook. She's Katie's mother – the girl who saw Father Thomas in the vestry."

Mrs Rook gave David a distracted smile, then turned back to Gawaine. "So what can I do to help?"

David was hopeful that Gawaine had come up with another angle on that mysterious disappearance, but what his friend actually asked was quite different.

"Mrs Rook, what can you tell me about Chantal Dupont?"

For a moment, Jennifer Rook looked completely taken aback. "But what can she have to do with anything?" she asked. "It must be almost two years since she left the village."

"Even so..." Gawaine murmured, waiting attentively.

"Well..." Mrs Rook hesitated, and to David's surprise she seemed almost embarrassed. "It wasn't a pleasant episode, and I don't really want to talk about it. But if you think it matters..."

"It might," Gawaine told her. "I know that she opened a beauty salon here. 'Skin Deep', it was called, I believe."

"That's right," Mrs Rook replied. " I thought it was a good idea. There's nothing like that closer than Guildford."

"But the business failed," Gawaine prompted her. "Why was that?"

Mrs Rook looked even more embarrassed. "Chantal didn't really get on with people," she explained. "It wasn't anything she did, but...well, she didn't have much in common with most of the people here. I mean, if someone

149

goes around in four inch heels and white capri pants, and full make-up at ten in the morning, in a place like Ellingwood…she's going to be looked at."

"She sounds like a good advertisement for her services," David said.

"I suppose so." Mrs Rook shifted uncomfortably. "There were rumours going round, too. That she…well, that she entertained men. I didn't believe it myself," she finished defensively.

"And where did the rumours come from?" Gawaine asked.

Jennifer Rook flushed. "I have my suspicions, but I'm not prepared to say. It wouldn't be fair."

"So people didn't like the look of her, and they believed the rumours, so they didn't patronize her business," Gawaine mused.

"It wasn't everyone!" Mrs Rook protested. "Stella Bretton went to her, I believe. And she gave me a shampoo and set when Hugo – that's my husband – had a work do, but I couldn't afford to go regularly."

"But enough people were put off..?"

"I suppose so," Mrs Rook said. "Christabel was very disapproving."

Why am I not surprised? David thought.

"She said it was just encouraging her behaviour if we went there," Jennifer Rook said. She hesitated, then went on with a rush, rather like a diver taking the plunge from a high board. "There was something else. Chantal wanted to start an aerobics class, here in the church hall. But our letting secretary told her there weren't any slots available, and I know that was a flat-out lie!"

"And who is the letting secretary?" Gawaine asked.

"Louise Braid."

David realised that in the last few minutes the piano music had stopped. Now the doors of the hall opened and a crowd of children straggled out into the car park.

"There's Katie," Mrs Rook said. "I've got to go."

She sounded relieved; David had the idea that she had said rather more than she felt comfortable about.

"Thank you," Gawaine said, stepping back. "You've been very helpful."

Mrs Rook hurried off, then turned back to ask, "You won't tell anyone what I told you, will you?"

Gawaine shook his head. "Don't worry about it."

"We'd better get going," David said, when Mrs Rook had finally departed. "Seff will think that we've fallen foul of the murderer."

"Mmm…"

Gawaine seemed abstracted as he got back into the car. "I knew there was something important about Chantal," he said while David started up the engine.

"It doesn't tell us anything about the murder," David pointed out. "It was all too long ago."

"I know, my dear David," Gawaine responded. "But it does give us some very useful ideas about the motive. Read between the lines: Chantal was frozen out of the village because she didn't meet with the approval of queen bees like Christabel. I don't for one minute believe that she was running a…a house of ill fame, though I can guess where the rumours came from."

"Oh?"

"Skin Deep is just opposite the doctor's surgery."

"I get it," David said. "Louise. It sounds as if Chantal was drop-dead gorgeous, so no wonder Louise didn't like her."

"Chantal's only problem was that she didn't fit in," Gawaine sighed. "A bird of paradise fluttering down among the pigeons."

"I don't get what a woman like that would want in Ellingwood in the first place," David said, halting at the car park entrance to let a lorry go by before nosing out into the road.

"Remember what Jennifer Rook said about her salon, my dear David. 'There's nothing like that closer than Guildford.' It could have worked."

"So you think that someone has a secret..?"

"That if it came to light, would mean they would go the way of Chantal Dupont," Gawaine finished for him. "Exactly."

The short journey to the centre of the village was already over; David found a parking place close to the Farrier's Arms.

"We'll discuss this later," he said.

"Yes, and for goodness' sake don't mention anything about it in front of Seff."

The autumn twilight had gathered; the air smelt smoky, as if from a nearby bonfire. The windows of the Farrier's Arms glowed a welcoming yellow. As they crossed the road to the entrance David watched Gawaine put on his social manner like an extra coat, and led the way inside.

Seff Brown was in the bar, in the company of a stunning African woman who was wearing a long caftan in a batik print. David rapidly revised his opinion of Father Thomas, seeing that he had managed to snaffle her as his fiancée.

Seff herself was looking as attractive as ever in a blue top and black silk trousers. David found himself regretting, not for the first time, that he and she would never get together. He wasn't even sure that he liked her, and he was pretty sure that she wasn't smitten with him. The jolt he felt on seeing her was purely physical.

"My dear Persephone!" Gawaine exclaimed. "It's good to see you. And Leah. Are you feeling better now?"

"Much better, thank you," Leah replied, managing a faint smile. "Miss Brown has been very kind."

"I keep telling you, my friends call me Seff." She gave David a nod, admitting him to the human race, and added, "Do you want a drink, or shall we go through? I think our table should be ready."

Since everyone elected to decamp to the restaurant, Seff led the way through an arch and into a long, narrow room, evidently an extension to the original pub, with a pointed glass roof like a large conservatory. Potted ferns and palms separated the tables.

A waiter showed Seff and the others to a table at one side of the room. At this time there were few other diners, though David spotted several woman at a long table down the far end, studying menus with much laughter and chat.

"Girls' night out," Seff murmured.

Another couple whom David had never seen before were seated opposite, and just beyond them Henry and Beryl Hartley were sipping drinks.

David touched Gawaine's arm and nodded towards the Hartleys. "Your suspects get everywhere."

Gawaine gave an elegant shrug. "My dear David, the Hartleys have every right to enjoy a peaceful night out. I intend to put all this out of my mind for the next couple of hours."

David didn't believe a word of that. He knew very well that nothing would put the murder out of Gawaine's mind until it was solved.

"Before you do that, Gawaine," Seff said, "let me just tell you about the cross. DCI Ferris okayed publicity, and my piece should be in the paper tomorrow morning. With your drawing. It's here, by the way." She fished in her bag and handed the sheet of paper back to Gawaine.

"That may stir up something," Gawaine murmured, sliding the drawing into an inside pocket. "Although I have to admit, I'm not hopeful."

"I played up Leah's angle," Seff continued. "How she gave Father Thomas the cross, how important it is to her, and so on. If the murderer still has it, he might be moved to return it."

"If he has any decency at all," Gawaine agreed.

David couldn't restrain a snort. "This is a murderer we're talking about."

"Nevertheless... People are very strange, my dear David. Who knows what might turn up?"

They were interrupted at that moment by the waiter appearing to take their drinks order, and for the next few minutes everyone was busy looking at the menu. Once that was dealt with and their drinks delivered, no one wanted to return to the topic of murder. Seff drew Leah deftly into the conversation, asking her about African food, and from there to life in general in Sierra Leone.

"My home is in Freetown," Leah said, "but working for the Nazareth Trust, I spend most of my time in upcountry villages. Life can be very hard there. There is much poverty."

"And the Trust was helping with that," Gawaine said.

Leah nodded. "We are building schools, hospitals, providing advice about crops…"

Less than riveted, David let his attention wander, and spotted a waiter ushering two more people into the restaurant. Malcolm Braid and his sister Louise.

Malcolm nodded as the waiter led them past. Louise seemed not to have noticed them, paying more attention to the couple seated opposite, the ones David didn't recognise. She halted by their table.

"Greg, how nice to see you!" she exclaimed. "Are the kiddies letting you have a night out?"

It was the woman who replied; David noticed how attractive she was, in a quiet, unassuming way, with dark auburn hair in a sleek cap, and a dress of soft green wool with here and there a touch of discreet gold jewellery. Louise, in contrast had her hair frizzed up unbecomingly, and she was wearing a coat in a garish shade of electric blue.

"The children are away, Louise." The woman's voice was arctic. "They've gone to stay with their grandparents for a few days."

"How lovely for you." Louise was either unaware of the other woman's hostility, or didn't care. "To have the house to yourselves for a while."

"I quite enjoy having my children around, thank you," the other woman responded.

"That's Dr Jerrold and his wife," Seff whispered; she was all ears, David noticed, obviously hoping to harvest a few grains for her paper. "Louise Braid works for him."

Now David remembered what Gawaine had told him, the gossip he had picked up from Mrs Prestwick in the church. According to her, Louise Braid, the doctor's receptionist, was infatuated with her employer.

No chance, David thought, eyeing the much more attractive Mrs Jerrold.

Half turning her back on Mrs Jerrold, Louise spoke again to the doctor. "I've updated Mrs Robson's details, and emailed the file to you."

"Thanks, Louise." Dr Jerrold spoke for the first time. His words were rapid and he sounded a bit embarrassed; David guessed he just wanted Louise to go away. "I'll get to it in the morning."

Louise leant over the doctor and touched him on the arm. "And you'll find something else on your desk, too," she said confidingly. "Something a bit special."

Amy Jerrold looked startled and affronted at Louise's words, while the doctor seemed even more embarrassed. "Er…thanks," he said.

Seff let out a long breath. "Is she out of her tiny mind?" Leaning over to murmur into David's ear, she added, "What's the 'something special', do you suppose?"

"Chocolate," David said firmly, trying hard to banish more esoteric speculation.

"You work so hard, Greg," Louise was continuing, apparently oblivious of the simmering Amy, or of her brother Malcolm, who was vainly trying to get her attention from the other side of the restaurant. "You deserve – "

"For goodness' sake!" Amy Jerrold had snapped at last, rising to her feet and spitting the words out. "Louise, can't you let us have a simple evening out without pushing in and interfering?"

"But I'm not – " Louise began to protest.

Amy over-rode her. "You're Greg's receptionist, but you've no idea what a proper working relationship should be. You're always overstepping. Discussing personal stuff. Giving him little presents. You even bring the kids sweets they shouldn't be having, and get them to call you Aunty Louise. Don't think I don't know what you're up to. But there's no chance of it, do you hear me? No chance! Greg, tell her!"

The doctor, appealed to, looked at both women with an expression of utter horror. "Amy, this isn't the time or the place..." he began helplessly.

"And what does Louise care about the time or the place?" Amy demanded. "Don't you dare take her side. I'm telling you, Greg, I've had enough. Either she goes, or I go."

"Amy, I can't..." the doctor began.

"I mean it," Amy said. "Her or me. Your choice."

"Greg, don't listen to her," Louise pleaded.

The doctor sat frozen for an eternal moment, then seemed to pull himself together. "Louise, take a couple of days off. Come in on Monday and we'll discuss this."

"You can't sack me!" Louise exclaimed. "You need me!"

"Louise, I told you." Dr Jerrold had managed to recover some authority in his tone. "We'll talk on Monday. Now please leave us alone to have our meal."

The girls' night out at the far table had fallen utterly silent. Those seated with their backs to the Jerrolds had twisted around to get a better look. The Hartleys too were watching the unfolding drama with interest.

Louise suddenly realised that she had an audience. Gazing around wildly, she cried out, "What are you all staring at?" Then she turned, sobs spilling out of her, and dashed out of the restaurant. She pushed her way through the crowds in the adjacent bar, and was gone.

Malcolm Braid hurried after her, tossing off an indiscriminate, "Sorry!" as he went.

The whole room seemed to relax when they had left. Gradually the level of chatter rose again; the girls' night out had their heads together over the table.

Amy Jerrold sat down; David could see that her hands were shaking and she looked as if she might burst into tears. Clearly she hadn't enjoyed the scene, even though she had been left in possession of the field – or the doctor. The two of them talked together in low voices.

"Well, *that* was interesting," Seff said.

Leah and Gawaine were both looking shocked, though David thought that Gawaine at least should have been prepared for passions to erupt in a village where someone had been stressed enough to commit murder. But he couldn't see that the scene they had just witnessed could have anything to do with the death of Father Thomas.

A moment later, a woman got up from the girls' night out table and walked over to the Jerrolds. David eyed her appreciatively. Though middle-aged, she was slender and well-groomed, with sleek blonde hair and a cream-coloured dress that only achieved such simple perfection by being extremely expensive. She bent over Amy Jerrold with one hand on her shoulder, and spoke quietly to her.

The only words David could catch were, "Nobody blames you."

"That's Stella Bretton," Seff said. "The headmaster's wife. I met her, just briefly, last Sunday, when she and her husband were coming away from Christabel Cottesmore's party. A very smooth number, I thought."

"She seems friendly with Mrs Jerrold," Gawaine remarked.

Amy Jerrold was beginning to cheer up as the two women talked. Eventually Stella Bretton patted her shoulder and went back to her own table.

At that moment, the waiter arrived with food. David was very glad to shrug off the aftermath of Louise Braid's hysterics, and concentrate on his meal. Gawaine, he realised, was doing the same, and deliberately steering the conversation away from the fracas.

The Jerrolds ate quickly and left. By the time David and the others had reached the stage of ordering coffee, the Hartleys too had gone, and the girls' night out were collecting their wraps and handbags, preparing to head out, from the sound of it, to the bar. As they streamed past, Seff rose and intercepted Stella Bretton.

"Mrs Bretton, could I have a word, please?"

Stella Bretton stared at her, eyes slightly narrowed, her attitude clearly hostile. "What? You're that reporter, aren't you? No, I've absolutely no intention of talking to you."

Gawaine had also risen to his feet. "I'm sorry to interrupt your evening, Mrs Bretton," he said. "But it really would be helpful if you could answer a few questions. I promise you, whatever you say will be confidential."

Seff let out an exasperated sigh, rolling her eyes, then sat down again with a thump. "Have it your way, Gawaine."

While Mrs Bretton still hesitated, Leah leant forward. "I believe you could help us find out who killed Tom," she said.

Stella Bretton cast a glance after her friends; through the archway David could see them clustering around the bar. Then she let out a long sigh and nodded. "I suppose so," she said ungraciously.

Gawaine found a chair for her, and signalled to the waiter for more coffee. "Mrs Bretton," he began, "on the Sunday morning that Father Thomas disappeared, your husband says that he was in his office going over some school accounts. Did you happen to see him there?"

Mrs Bretton paused before she answered, fiddling with the links of a gold bracelet on her right wrist. "In other words, can I give John an alibi?" she said at last. "And since I can't be made to testify against him, I'll answer that. No, I can't. I didn't see him all morning."

"You didn't even take him a cup of coffee?" David asked.

Mrs Bretton gave him an unfriendly look. She was perfectly self-possessed, apparently unmoved by the thought that her husband might be a murderer.

"He was in the school office," she explained. "I was in our house, across the playing fields from the main school buildings. So, no, I didn't take him coffee. And our daughter Emma sings in the church choir, so she can't give him an alibi, either. But I've absolutely no doubt that John was where he said he was. He had no reason to want Father Thomas dead."

"The trouble at the school...?" Gawaine began delicately.

"Sell all that you have and give it to the poor?" Stella Bretton let out a short puff of laughter. "That was farcical," she said. "And John was quite capable of making sure that it didn't happen again, without needing to kill the wretched man."

"And what about you?" Seff asked. Although her tone was neutral, David got the idea that she wasn't too keen on the stylish and soignée Mrs Bretton. "Did you have any reason to want Father Thomas dead?"

Stella Bretton raised her brows. "Whyever should I?" She picked up her coffee cup and took a sip, her hand perfectly steady.

"Well..." Seff shrugged. "If he had found out about you and Andrew Danby, for example."

For an eyeblink, Mrs Bretton looked furious. David wouldn't have been surprised if she had thrown her coffee into Seff's face. But a moment later she had herself under control again. She set down her cup and spoke quietly.

"You've been talking to Mrs Prestwick. Terrible old gossip."

"Actually, I spoke to Mrs Prestwick too," Gawaine said. Looking acutely embarrassed, he added, "Is what she said true?"

"Oh, we had a fling," Stella Bretton confessed. "But that's all it was. To tell you the truth, I'm bored out of my mind in Ellingwood. I was never cut out to be a headmaster's wife."

"So you alleviated your boredom by going to bed with Andrew Danby?" Seff asked.

161

"For a while. I ended it."

"Really? Why?"

Stella Bretton met Seff's interested gaze. "Because I didn't like the way he talked about Marjorie. I know I was unfaithful to John sexually, but I've always been loyal to him in other ways. Andrew just wanted to sneer at his wife the whole time. I got fed up with it."

"He wasn't worried that you would tell Marjorie what he said?" David asked.

Stella shook her head, amused. "He thought I was in love with him, the poor worm. Besides, Marjorie wouldn't have believed me. She thinks the sun shines out of him."

"And what if Father Thomas had found out?" Seff persisted.

Mrs Bretton shrugged. "It didn't matter to me, whether he knew or not."

"But if he told your husband?"

Stella tipped her head to one side, considering. "Do you know, I'm not sure. But John and I have a very good understanding. I can't imagine that it would have been too dreadful. Certainly not worth committing murder for."

David flashed a glance at Gawaine. He was concentrating intently on Mrs Bretton, and it was hard to tell what he thought about what she was telling him.

"But Andrew Danby might have committed murder?" he suggested.

Again Stella Bretton thought about that for a moment before replying. "He might well," she said at last, "though frankly I don't think he has the guts for it. You know that it's Marjorie who has the money, I suppose?"

Gawaine nodded. "I'm surprised he takes the risk."

"Oh, I suppose he thinks Marjorie would forgive him if she ever found out," Stella responded. "He has such a good opinion of himself. Thinks he's God's gift to women; I don't imagine for one moment that I was the only pebble on his beach."

Gawaine looked pained. David felt a jolt of surprise. He would never have pegged Danby, physically or in his personality, as a successful stud, though he could visualise him leering from afar. *He must have a very good technique.*

"You'd be surprised what goes on in Ellingwood," Stella Bretton went on. "Though I wouldn't have expected any of it to lead to murder. But none of us – especially the women – have enough to do. I was much happier in Hereford, where we lived before this. I had my own business there."

"Really?" said Seff.

"A boutique. I sold posh frocks, designer knitwear, bits of jewellery…you know the kind of thing." Her tone grew wistful. "I loved my little shop, and it was doing well. But then John was offered the headship here, and it would have been lunatic to turn it down. So I had to sell up. I still miss it – it was so much more fun than endless coffee mornings and bridge parties."

"And going to bed with Andrew Danby," Seff added.

"God, yes!"

"You know," Gawaine said meditatively, "there should be an opening for another little shop, in Guildford, maybe, or Reigate. Here in Ellingwood, even."

Stella gave him a look of surprise. "I thought about that once, but…maybe I'll think about it again. So." She rose to her feet. "If that's everything, I think I'll go and join my friends."

"Thank you," Gawaine said. "You've been very helpful."

Stella gave him a nod, then walked off to where the other women were still sitting in the bar. She trailed expensive perfume as she went.

David glanced across at Gawaine. "Trying to save her marriage?"

"It wasn't her marriage I had in mind, my dear David," Gawaine responded.

"So what do you think?" Leah asked. She had remained silent throughout the conversation, but she had been focused and alert, taking in every word. "Did she kill Tom? Did her husband?"

"I'd discount her," Gawaine replied thoughtfully. "I don't think she would have had the physical strength to lug a body around. John Bretton now…it all depends on whether Mrs Bretton was telling the truth when she said that he could have stopped Father Thomas interfering with the school. I must remember to check that."

"And Andrew Danby?" Seff asked.

"Andrew Danby has an alibi," Gawaine reminded her. "He and his wife were in church."

"We really ought to check up on that too," David said. What he had just heard had made him even keener to pin the murder on Danby.

"Maybe," Gawaine said, and refused to be drawn any further.

Chapter Seventeen

…the unsatiable avarice of such as sought more their own
lucre, than the glory of God.

Of Ceremonies

Gawaine intended to leave for Ellingwood the following
morning to tackle DCI Ferris over the questioning of
Richard Coates. But as he was closing the front door behind
him, a taxi turned in at his gate. Susan Cox got out of it,
paid the driver, and met Gawaine at the bottom of his steps.

"I have to talk to you," she said. "They've arrested
Richard."

Gawaine wondered how many more distraught
females were likely to accost him over the course of this
investigation. He wished once again that David had not
already departed for his day of honest toil, since his friend
coped much better with this sort of thing.

Susan Cox looked haggard, ten years older than when
she had arrived with Leah on the previous day. Gawaine
guessed she hadn't slept since then.

"Come in," he said. "Tell me what happened."

He led Susan through to the conservatory. This
time she was blind to the beauty of the orchids and the
bougainvillaea, sitting on the edge of her chair and leaning
forward with her hands tightly clasped.

"They came to the hotel yesterday and took Richard in for questioning," she began. "I went with him, to Guildford police station, not the incident room in Ellingwood. Of course they didn't let me sit in on the questioning. I thought they must have got hold of Tom's will, since it put Richard in control of the company."

"That does give him a motive," Gawaine observed, taking the chair opposite her.

"Yes, but it's all so ridiculous! As if Richard and I ever argued...but I suppose the police don't know that. All the same, I expected it would all be over quite quickly."

"And it wasn't?"

"No, it went on and on. I waited there all night. Then early this morning DCI Ferris came to tell me that they had charged Richard with Tom's murder!" There was fear in her eyes as she looked at Gawaine. "I know he didn't do it!"

Gawaine met her gaze thoughtfully. "They didn't question you at all?"

Susan shook her head. "No, but Ferris told me not to leave the area." When Gawaine made no response she added, "We have to do something!"

Gawaine took a breath, wondering if Susan was lying to him by omission, or whether she really had no idea of what might have gone on in that interview room.

"They wouldn't have arrested him purely on the matter of the will," he said at last. "What about his alibi? Is there no one to vouch for his being in Manchester on that Sunday morning?"

"No, because he wasn't in Manchester." Susan twisted her fingers together. "He was in London."

166

"Oh?"

"He drove down on the previous Wednesday for an auction," Susan explained. "You know about our business – Oriental antiques and curios? Mostly we import from the Far East, but we also pick up pieces at auction in this country. There was an auction at Sotheby's on the Thursday and Friday of that week, and Richard attended, and bought a few items there."

"Which would be well documented," Gawaine said. "What happened on the Saturday?"

"Richard stayed over to visit some friends," Susan replied. "He had dinner with them, then went back to his hotel and checked out on the Sunday morning."

"You don't know what time?" Gawaine asked, then added, "No, never mind that. The police will have found out from the hotel. It must have been early enough for him to get down here and kill Father Thomas, or they wouldn't have arrested him."

"But he didn't do it!" There was a sob in Susan's voice. "You have to believe that."

Gawaine stretched out a hand, a calming gesture, though he didn't touch Susan. "That is the premise I'm working on," he assured her. "But we won't get anywhere unless we can construct the police case against him."

Susan's shoulders sagged. "I suppose not."

"So I suppose your brother drove back to Manchester that Sunday," Gawaine went on. "Do you know what time he arrived?"

"Late," Susan admitted reluctantly. "Eleven or so. Caroline – that's his wife – rang me because she was getting worried, and she wanted to know if he'd been in touch

167

with me. Then Richard turned up while she was on the phone. He said there had been a pile-up on the motorway; he wasn't involved, but the traffic was backed up for miles and then diverted along country roads."

"The police will be able to check if that's true," Gawaine murmured.

"I know it was true," Susan retorted. "I'd watched the news that night and it was on there. That's the main reason that Caroline – Richard's wife – was worried."

Gawaine nodded, aware that even though the accident had happened, there was no proof that Richard had been held up by it. But it was a very convenient coincidence if he had indeed been in Surrey killing his brother.

"Richard didn't phone his wife?" he asked.

"Caroline said not," Susan replied. "I don't know why."

Gawaine considered that. If Richard had been industriously establishing an alibi, he would have been more likely to phone than not. An innocent man might have been so intent on getting home that phoning had slipped his mind.

"Leah told me that the police took your car," he said, shelving the question of the alibi for the time being. "Was that – ?"

"You've seen Leah?" Susan half stood up, then slumped back into her chair. "I went back to the hotel to shower and change, and she wasn't there. I'd no idea where she'd gone."

"She came here," Gawaine told her.

"And she's here now? I need to tell her – "

Gawaine stretched out a hand again, this time to silence Susan. "She's staying at the Farrier's Arms in Ellingwood.

A friend of mine is looking after her. And I really don't think it would be a good idea for you to see her just now."

Susan stared at him as if she was having trouble understanding what he meant. Then she let out a long sigh. "I see. Yes, you're right. But it doesn't stop me worrying about her. I don't want her going back to Africa thinking that Richard killed Tom."

"Then we need to sort this out quickly," Gawaine responded, though privately wondering whether his instincts might be wrong and Richard Coates had indeed murdered his brother. "Tell me about the car," he added.

"I don't know anything for certain." Susan was obviously having trouble focusing. "I assume they took it to check for any traces that Richard..." Her voice shook and she had to stop.

"That Richard used it to transport his brother's body," Gawaine finished for her, trying to push aside the unpleasant picture that the words called up. "But I assume Father Thomas must have been a passenger in the car. Any traces could be quite innocent."

Susan had turned her head away and pressed a hand over her mouth. Gawaine waited, until a few moments later she took a breath and faced him again, clearly making a massive effort to control herself.

"No, it's worse than that. When Tom came back from Africa last March, Richard and I went to meet him at the airport, using Richard's car. It was a freezing cold day. Tom only had lightweight clothing, and he was stick thin from the malaria. He couldn't stop shivering, even with the heating on. So I bundled him up in these two old travelling rugs that Richard keeps in the boot in case he has to transport fragile pieces. And afterwards the rugs went back into the boot."

"Oh…" Gawaine began to feel even more uncertain. Traces of Father Thomas in the boot of the car were far more incriminating than anything else he had heard so far. There was an innocent explanation, but would the police believe it? *Do I believe it? Transporting fragile antiques rolled up in a rug sounds frightfully cavalier to me…*

But faced with Richard Coates's sister, distressed as she was, Gawaine found it quite impossible to admit that he might be wrong. "I'll get in touch with DCI Ferris," he said, "and see if he'll tell me exactly what is going on."

"Oh, thank you…"

"And meanwhile," Gawaine continued, "may I suggest you go back to your hotel and rest. I have your number if I need to talk to you again."

Susan hesitated, clearly reluctant.

"You have told me everything..?" Gawaine prompted her gently.

"Everything I know. It's just…oh, I know it's no good going over it all again and again. But I feel as if I ought to be doing something more."

"These things take time," Gawaine said. "Just leave it with me."

This time Susan saw the sense in what he was telling her, and left without any more protest. Gawaine drove her to the station where she could catch a train for Guildford, but in the car she was silent. Clearly she was locked into her own worries, and Gawaine wished vainly for some magic word that would help.

On his way home he stopped to buy a copy of Seff's paper, and was pleased to see that her piece about Father Thomas's cross, along with his drawing, had a prominent place on an inside page. Then he reflected how unlikely it was that the cross would turn up again.

It would be a miracle if it did, he thought. The recovery of the cross would be a tiny consolation for Leah, and might point away from Richard Coates, depending on where it was found. *Dear Lord, we need a miracle.*

When Gawaine let himself back into his house, the telephone was ringing. It was the bishop's secretary.

"We have the results of the audit of St Paul's accounts," she told Gawaine. "Everything is perfectly all right."

"Really?"

"Really. 'Meticulously accurate' was the term the auditor used. Would you like a copy of the report?"

"No, thank you." Gawaine shuddered at the thought of trying to make sense of a balance sheet. "But there is another thing you might be able to help me with."

The secretary made an encouraging noise.

"Do you know – or can you find out – if there's any legal reason why the vicar of St Paul's is the chaplain to Ellingwood Court school?"

"I don't know offhand," the secretary replied. Gawaine could sense her curiosity fizzing down the telephone wires. "But I can find out for you."

Gawaine thanked her and rang off. *Another motive bites the dust,* he thought, mentally removing Henry and Beryl Hartley from his list of suspects. *And maybe now I can settle John Bretton, one way or another.*

Gawaine left his car once again in the church hall car park and headed for the incident room at the back of the hall. But when he arrived the first person he spotted was Christabel, standing in the doorway and rattling her church keys impatiently.

"What do *you* want?" she asked disagreeably.

Gawaine winced inwardly, but summoned the soft answer that in Christabel's case was rarely sufficient to turn away wrath. "I came to talk to DCI Ferris."

"Well, you're out of luck. The police have made an arrest and they're finishing up here."

Christabel stepped back so that Gawaine could see past her into the room, where two uniformed officers were packing up the paraphernalia of their investigation. One was loading files into plastic crates, while the other collected detritus into a black sack.

"I'd better not find one single cigarette end when you've finished," Christabel called to him.

"We've never smoked in here, madam," the officer replied stolidly.

Christabel made the sound normally rendered as, "Tcha!" To Gawaine, she added, "So you can go back to your flowers and your drawing or whatever it is you do with your time. I can't imagine what the point was of bringing you here in the first place."

So why did you? Gawaine thought. Aloud he said, "I still need to talk to DCI Ferris."

The file-loading officer heard what he said and walked over toward him. "I'm sorry, sir, but DCI Ferris is back in Guildford now. Would you like to speak to him on the phone?"

172

"Yes, thank you."

Gawaine reached into the inside pocket where he had stowed Ferris's card, but before he could find it the officer slid a phone out of his top pocket, punched in a number and handed the phone to Gawaine, who retreated with it into the car park, followed by a baleful glare from Christabel.

"Ferris." Gawaine almost dropped the phone as the voice barked into his ear. As soon as he identified himself, the DCI went on, "We charged Richard Coates this morning. So I think we can say it's all wrapped up. Thank you for your help, sir."

Insincerity oozed out of his voice on the last few words.

"I beg your pardon, Chief Inspector," Gawaine said, "but I can't help thinking that it isn't wrapped up at all. Richard Coates – "

"Richard Coates had a good motive for killing his brother," Ferris interrupted, "he has no alibi for that Sunday morning, and there are traces of his brother's body in the boot of his car. What more do you want?"

"Mrs Cox explained to me about the car – "

Ferris let out a snort. "Oh, you've spoken to her? Right. Well, Coates explained it to me, but they would, wouldn't they?"

"And the churchwardens' staves?"

"Clean."

Gawaine wasn't sure what to say next. The case against Richard Coates looked very black. And he had nothing to set against the evidence except his own conviction that the man was innocent.

"So if that's all, sir…"

"No, it's not all," Gawaine said, desperation fuelling him. "What about Father Thomas's missing cross?"

"What about it? You know as well as I do that it's destroyed. But if it'll make you happy..." His voice took on the tone of someone humoring a recalcitrant two-year-old. "We're liaising with the Manchester police. They're sending a team to search Coates's property. If the cross is there, they'll find it. We think we have a handle on the murder weapon, too."

"Oh?" Gawaine felt a spark of interest – not a pleasant one, if this was another piece of evidence against Richard.

"Yes. At that auction he went to, Coates bought a Tibetan incense burner – basically a brass pot with knobs on. You could do a lot of damage with one of those. The Manchester police will impound it and get it tested."

Gawaine tried and failed to call up a picture of Richard Coates swiping his brother with a Tibetan incense burner. It was too far outside the realms of possibility.

"Have you any more questions?" Ferris asked impatiently.

"Not for the moment." Gawaine ignored the heavy sigh that greeted these words. "Thank you, Chief Inspector."

The call was abruptly cut off. Gawaine returned to the hall to give the phone back to its owner, and wished Christabel a polite goodbye before driving away.

Richard Coates did not do this murder, he thought stubbornly. *But the police won't be looking for anyone else, not now. So it's up to me. And I haven't the remotest idea of what to do next.*

Chapter Eighteen

Break not the bruised reed, nor quench the smoking flax.
The Visitation of the Sick

David Powers was worried. When he arrived from work on Thursday evening, he found Gawaine deeply anxious over the arrest of Richard Coates. David, who was perfectly willing to believe that Coates was guilty, could not convince Gawaine that the case was over and he could stop driving himself crazy.

"The police are focused on Richard Coates now," Gawaine explained fretfully over supper. "They haven't been in touch with me again, and why should they? As far as they're concerned, they've caught a murderer."

"Maybe they have," David said.

Gawaine shook his head. He was looking tired and strained. "I've tried to make myself believe that, and I can't. But I don't know what to do next." He toyed unenthusiastically with Mrs Summers' delicious crab mousse. "All my leads have come to dead ends."

"Are you sure?" David asked. "What about John Bretton?"

"Oh – yes, I didn't tell you about that. The bishop's secretary called me back. Apparently the tradition that the vicar of St Paul's acts as chaplain to Ellingwood Court goes back to the incumbent before Jim Trask, and the previous Head of the school. But there's nothing in writing."

"So nothing to stop John Bretton from telling Father Thomas never to darken his door again?"

"Nothing at all," Gawaine said, with another prod at the inoffensive crab.

"Hey, but wait a minute," David said. "Suppose Bretton is like Andrew Danby? Handing you a weak motive in the hope of covering up something more serious?"

A faint spark of interest showed in Gawaine's expression. "Possible. Though if so, he's covering it up remarkably well."

"Then there's Andrew Danby himself," David went on, slightly encouraged that Gawaine was at least discussing things. "We still haven't questioned him about his affair with Stella Bretton."

Gawaine's mouth quirked into a look of distaste. "Nor need we. Stella Bretton told us all about it. And Andrew Danby has an alibi. He was in church."

"Maybe we should check that." David felt that he was repeating himself.

"Maybe." Gawaine gave a dispirited shrug. "But I'm sure it would be a waste of time."

"And what about the rest of the congregation? There could be plenty of people with guilty secrets we know nothing about."

Gawaine smiled wearily. "Oh, of course, my dear David. And how do you propose we investigate that. 'Excuse me, but would you mind telling me what you're hiding?' I can't imagine that would be very productive. Besides," he went on, "I think we can discount the ordinary members of the congregation. Barring some extreme criminal act, they might not be too worried if their guilty secrets came to light. At least, not to the point of murder. No, my dear David, we're looking for someone deeply invested in the life of the church and the village. Somebody whose life would change substantially if their reputation were ruined. Somebody who doesn't want to be the next Chantal."

"Someone with a business, then, like the doctor or Malcolm Braid?"

"Maybe, though Dr Jerrold has no motive, and Malcolm Braid has an alibi. But it doesn't have to be a matter of business. Just someone with a comfortable life, nice house, friends…"

David snorted. "Christabel's little lot."

"Exactly."

"Someone with a role to play in the church, like the treasurer or the churchwardens," David mused. He wondered whether anyone would really commit a murder to hang onto a job like that, then reflected that in ultra-respectable Ellingwood, they very well might. *It's not only the job. It's the reputation that goes with it.* "What about the organist? No one has mentioned him."

"Her," Gawaine corrected him. "No, the organist would be playing before the service started – at the very time Father Thomas was disappearing."

David made a dissatisfied noise. "Suppose she set up something to play the organ automatically? Then she sneaks away…"

He was gratified to see a spark of amusement in Gawaine's eyes. "With a life-size automaton to take her

177

place, my dear David? In St Paul's, the organist sits in full view of the congregation."

"Pity," David said. "But hang on – aren't we missing something here," he went on after a moment. "We should look these people up on the criminal records register – and the sex offender's register, come to that."

Gawaine gave him a pained look. "The police will have done that, surely?"

"Of course. But they're not telling us about it, are they?

Gawaine hesitated, looking unhappy once again. David knew that he would regard searching for someone's iniquities online as appallingly ill-mannered, something like snooping through private correspondence.

But there are times when it's necessary to snoop.

Eventually Gawaine gave a decided shake of his head.

"Oh, come on!" David protested before his friend could speak. "I know you think it's unsporting – "

"That's not the point," Gawaine interrupted. "Don't you see, my dear David, that if the guilty secret is out there in…er…in cyberspace, then anyone could find it out, and there would be no point in killing Father Thomas to *keep* it secret. Besides, anyone with a role to play in the church would have had to go through the usual background check."

David reluctantly had to admit that Gawaine was right. "So what we're looking for," he said, "is a criminal or a sex offender who has managed to get away with it. So far."

Gawaine frowned, dissatisfied. "Maybe, but it doesn't have to be that serious. Remember Chantal. She hadn't done anything wrong, except to transgress the codes of Ellingwood, and look what happened to her."

David murmured agreement, but he wasn't at all certain in his own mind. He decided that as soon as he got the chance he would search for their suspects on the appropriate websites, whether Gawaine liked it or not.

But when he did that, later that evening, he found what Gawaine had told him he would find: precisely nothing.

On Friday morning, Gawaine was up so early that David suspected he hadn't slept all night. He was looking positively ill, drifting around the house from study to sitting room to conservatory, to the music room where he played a few random notes on the clavichord and drifted back through the hall towards the sitting room again.

"You're driving me mad!" David exclaimed from where he sat in the dining room finishing breakfast. "For goodness' sake settle to something."

Gawaine paused at the door and looked David in the eye. "Such as..?"

"Well, suppose we sit down and go over the whole thing from start to finish."

Gawaine looked even more distressed. "We can't. You're supposed to go to work."

"Not a problem." David shrugged. "I can call in to take the day off."

"But that – " Gawaine broke off at the sound of the telephone, went to answer it and came back a moment later. David stared at him. He was animated, bright-eyed, his depression vanished.

"That was Seff," he said. "I have to get over to Ellingwood right away. The cross has turned up. In the words of the master, my dear David, the game's afoot!"

"Then I'm definitely coming with you." David swallowed the last of his coffee. "If this thing is going to break, I want to be there. Give me a minute to phone."

"Where?" David asked, when they were in the car and heading towards Ellingwood.

"The Farrier's Arms," Gawaine replied. "And, to coin a phrase, step on it. I'd like to get there before the police."

David obligingly stepped on it, ignoring a faint whimper of terror from his passenger. When they drew up outside the Farrier's Arms there was no sign of a police car.

It was still too early for the pub to be open, but Seff was waiting at the side door, beckoning Gawaine and David inside. Following Gawaine into the bar, David found Leah Koroma there, sitting at a table and looking as if she might burst into tears at any moment. The landlord was standing behind the bar, gazing at an ebony and silver cross set on the bar in front of him. A padded bag lay discarded nearby.

Gawaine took in the scene at a glance. "This is Father Thomas's cross?" he asked Leah, though David thought the question was unnecessary.

Leah nodded mutely.

"How did you find it?" Gawaine asked the landlord.

"I found it." For the first time David noticed an elderly woman in a blue cardigan and flowered pinny, standing in the shadows at the end of the bar. She was clutching a mop as if she might be about to take off on it.

"Mrs Prestwick." Gawaine turned towards her. "Please, tell me what happened."

"I was cleaning this morning, like always, and I found it on the shelf under the phone, just next to the gents. I'll show you if you like."

At Gawaine's murmured agreement, Mrs Prestwick led the way across the bar and through a door on the far side. It opened into a narrow passage with doors on either side leading to the lavatories. Through the glass door at the far end David could see the pub car park. In an alcove about half way down the passage was a public phone bolted to the wall; a shelf underneath it held a tattered phone directory.

"You found it here this morning?" Gawaine asked. "You're sure it wasn't there yesterday?"

"It was not." Mrs Prestwick's tone was downright. "I always check that shelf. You wouldn't believe what gets left there…pigs, some people are."

Gawaine nodded slowly. "So the cross was put there at some time after you cleaned yesterday, and before you cleaned today. Thank you, that's very helpful."

Returning to the bar, David saw that the police had arrived, in the person of a bullish plain clothes officer and a much younger, well-scrubbed sergeant. The landlord was repeating the story that Mrs Prestwick had just told them.

"DCI Ferris," Gawaine murmured to David, with a nod towards the older officer. "So far you've avoided the pleasure of his company."

David gathered that it might be just as well.

As they re-entered the bar, Ferris broke off what he was saying; his eyes narrowed when he spotted Gawaine. "I might have known you would be here," he said.

"So glad to oblige," Gawaine murmured.

Ferris snorted, and thereafter ignored Gawaine, striding across the bar to inspect the passage for himself, and then returning to question Mrs Prestwick about the timing.

"You're sure about that?" he demanded.

"Course I'm sure," Mrs Prestwick snapped back. "What do you take me for?"

"Mrs Prestwick is very thorough," the landlord put in. "If she says it wasn't there yesterday, it wasn't there."

"It won't have escaped your notice, Chief Inspector," Gawaine said silkily, "that in the time between the newspaper report about the cross, and its turning up here, Richard Coates was in police custody."

If looks could have killed, David thought, Gawaine might have been reduced to a pile of gently smoking ash. Then Ferris grunted. "Fair point." Turning back to the landlord, he asked, "How many people went down that passage?"

The landlord rolled his eyes. "It leads to the toilets," he pointed out in the tone of someone who explains the obvious to a backward three-year-old. "How many people do you think went down it?"

Ferris grunted again, clearly not pleased. "And how many people have handled that thing?" he asked, with a nod towards the cross.

"I handled the bag," Mrs Prestwick said. "But I never looked inside it. I handed it in, like I do with all the lost property."

"I touched the bag," the landlord added. "And the cross, just enough to take it out. And then I phoned you. No one else has been near it."

"Not even you?" DCI Ferris asked Leah.

"No." Leah's voice was shaking, but she met the Chief Inspector's gaze without flinching. "I know about fingerprints."

Gawaine had drawn closer to the bar, and was examining the cross and the bag as closely as he could without actually touching them. "There won't be any fingerprints, you know," he murmured. "The murderer isn't that stupid."

"And you won't be able to trace the bag," Seff put in. "That kind is sold all over the place."

Ferris gave her an unfriendly look, and David wondered whether she had been right to call attention to herself. The DCI could easily throw her out.

He had opened his mouth to speak when his mobile rang, cutting off whatever he had been about to say. Sliding it out of an inside pocket, he barked, "Ferris." For a few moments he listened, his expression growing suddenly intent. "What?" he demanded, and added a single word that made Gawaine wince. "Okay," he added. "I'm onto it."

Putting the phone away, Ferris turned to the landlord. "Where's the doctor's surgery?" he asked.

The landlord blinked in surprise, but answered readily. "Turn left out of here, then take the first left. It's a white building on the right, with a sign outside. You can't miss it."

Ferris was already making for the door. "Fingerprint these two," he said to his sergeant in passing. "And bag up the cross and the bag. Then come and find me."

"Hey, can I open – ?" the landlord called, but Ferris had already gone.

Seff followed him out, looking as if all her Christmases had come at once, while Gawaine and David brought up the rear.

"Now what?" David said.

Gawaine shrugged. He was looking a good deal happier than he had been for several days. "I have no idea," he replied. "But whatever it is, if it's connected to this case, it has to be good for Richard Coates. He has the best of all alibis."

DCI Ferris barrelled down the street, his entourage following. The white building the landlord had mentioned was two or three hundred yards from the pub, set back a little way from the street behind a low wall. Tubs of geraniums flanked the main door on either side.

As Ferris and the others approached, David heard the two-tone note of a siren growing rapidly louder. An ambulance appeared from the opposite direction and halted outside the surgery to disgorge two paramedics.

At the same moment a second door at the far end of the building burst open. Malcolm Braid staggered out to meet the paramedics and pointed behind him towards the open door; David saw a flight of stairs leading upwards.

The paramedics vanished up the stairs at a run, and DCI Ferris followed more slowly. As he passed Malcolm Braid, he snapped out, "Stay here."

Braid looked after him for a moment, then sagged slowly at the knees and sank down onto the low wall.

"What happened?" Seff asked.

Braid looked up at her blankly, as if he had no idea who she was or what her question meant. His prominent blue eyes were glazed and his skin was pallid, sweating.

"What happened?" David repeated.

Braid seemed to make a massive effort to pull himself together. It was to Gawaine that he spoke. "It's Louise... She...she killed herself."

Chapter Nineteen

Thou knowest, Lord, the secrets of our hearts.
At the Burial of the Dead

Gawaine sat down beside Malcolm Braid on the low wall of the surgery. "Do you want to talk about it?" he asked.

Braid was silent for a moment, then jerked into speech. "I suppose I'll have to tell…" He gestured towards the door where DCI Ferris had disappeared. Then he let out a long sigh. "It's my fault. It's all my fault."

"Why?" David asked. "You didn't kill her, did you?"

Gawaine shot him a warning glance, but Braid seemed not to register the tactlessness of the question.

"I should have realised how upset she was…" he murmured, staring into space.

"Suppose you start at the beginning," Gawaine encouraged him. "Does this have anything to do with what happened in the restaurant on Wednesday night?"

Braid nodded. "Poor Louise… She couldn't really have expected that Greg Jerrold would have left Amy for her. But having it all spelt out in public like that… I suppose she couldn't take it."

David eased away, to leave the questioning to Gawaine, and spotted Seff in the background, unobtrusively taking notes. He wondered how long they had before Ferris came down to interrupt, and at the same time he asked himself whether this could possibly have any relevance to the murder of Father Thomas. Louise Braid and her pathetic attempt at a love affair couldn't have much to do with the dead priest.

"Louise worked for the doctor, didn't she?" Gawaine continued.

"Yes, she was his receptionist. And she lived in the flat above the surgery. After that row in the Farrier's Arms I took her home with me and she stayed over Wednesday night, but yesterday she wanted to come back." He banged a fist down on the rough brick top of the wall. "I should never have let her. But I didn't think she was as upset as all that…"

"And then…" Gawaine prompted.

"This morning I phoned her. I wanted to make sure she was okay, and I thought I might take some time off and drive her down to the coast, maybe for a long weekend… get her away from all the gossip for a bit. There was no reply, and when I tried again a bit later and she still didn't answer, I started to get worried." Braid was talking more coherently now, as if he was getting over the first shock. "I have a key – she has one of mine, too, we look after each other's place if we go away. I let myself in and I found her…" His voice shook and he wiped a hand over his forehead. "I found her in bed. She had a bag tied over her head…a black bin liner. God, it was horrible!"

Gawaine touched his shoulder sympathetically. "I'm sorry."

"She has some sleeping stuff the doctor gave her. The packet was beside her bed – empty. I pulled the bag off, but I could see it was no use. I called the ambulance, but I knew she'd gone."

"And you called the police too?" David asked, prepared to be tactless again.

Braid stared at him. "Of course. You know as well as I do that the police have to be informed about things like this."

Before Gawaine could respond, the paramedics reappeared, followed by Ferris, who walked over to Malcolm Braid.

"I'm sorry, Mr Braid," he said. "There was nothing the medics could do. And this is now a crime scene. I shall need to ask you some questions."

Gawaine looked confused. "But Chief Inspector...do you think that Louise Braid was murdered?"

Ferris gave him an unfriendly glance. "It *looks* like a straightforward suicide. But there's been one murder in this village already. I'm going to make damn' sure that this isn't another one." Turning back to Braid, he added, "Come back up to the flat, please. We can talk there."

Braid got to his feet and headed for the door to the stairs; David thought he looked reluctant to return to where his sister's body was lying. Ferris went up after him, hard on his heels like a sheepdog trying to herd one recalcitrant sheep.

"I have to send my story in," Seff said, flourishing her notebook as she headed into the street. "I'll see you later."

"Make sure Leah is all right," Gawaine called after her.

"Of course!" Seff tossed the words over her shoulder and hurried off towards the Farrier's Arms.

David and Gawaine followed more slowly. Instead of returning to the car, Gawaine drifted towards one of the benches on the village green, and sat in silence for a few minutes, watching the ducks on the pond.

"Well?" David prompted when the silence had started to get on his nerves.

Gawaine glanced at him, then quickly away again. His eyes were tragic. David knew that he was grieving for Louise Braid, even though he had seen little of her, and hadn't much liked her.

"It doesn't bear thinking about," he said after a moment. "Had she so little in her life that she couldn't go on, after what happened on Wednesday? It wasn't that important, surely?"

"It was pretty shattering," David contradicted him. "She was in love with Dr Jerrold and he rejected her. Amy Jerrold made it quite clear that she wasn't welcome in their lives. She might have lost her job, and the flat that went with it. And all that in public!"

Gawaine let out a long sigh. "I suppose so."

"Maybe she lived a rich fantasy life," David continued, "where the doctor's eyes were suddenly opened and he realised she was the one he'd loved all along. Or maybe her real life was enough for her: being at her beloved's beck and call, telling herself that his wife never did so much for him…"

"And all that gone," Gawaine murmured. "But was she so fragile that she couldn't face life any more? She wasn't quite alone; she had her brother. Should she really be dead? I wonder if she left a note," he added after a moment. "I should have asked."

"Most suicides do," David said. "So if there wasn't a note…"

"Indeed. It might suggest that she was murdered."

"Then who murdered her?" David asked.

Gawaine frowned thoughtfully. "There was no sign of a break-in," he began, "or someone would have mentioned it. Therefore Louise either let her murderer in, or he had a key."

"Her brother!" David was surprised.

"Murder is so often a family affair, my dear David. Though I think we can safely assume that Dr Jerrold also had a key."

"Or Mrs Jerrold," David added. "Oh, I like that."

"Getting rid of the hated rival? But really, Amy Jerrold can't have taken Louise seriously as a threat. Unless…" Gawaine's voice trailed off and he fell to contemplating the ducks once more.

"Look," David began, after the silence had once more stretched out for several minutes. "As I see it, there are three possibilities." He ticked them off on his fingers. "One, Louise killed herself because of the hassle with the doctor. Two, she was murdered by her brother for some unknown reason. Three, she was murdered by someone else altogether, with the doctor and his wife as front runners."

Gawaine considered. "You have forgotten possibility one(a), my dear David. Louise killed herself because she murdered Father Thomas and couldn't take the guilt any longer. Or she was afraid of being found out."

"You don't really think that!" David said, startled.

"No, I don't. But the sequence of events…Seff's piece about the cross comes out, the cross is returned, Louise

190

Braid kills herself. Are these events connected?" he asked with a pedantic air. "Or was that distressing scene in the restaurant and Louise's subsequent suicide completely irrelevant to Father Thomas's murder?"

"I've no idea," David confessed. "What do you think?"

"I incline towards your point three," Gawaine replied. "With a slight leaning towards point one."

"You don't like my point two, then?" David said. "That Braid killed her?"

"No…because why would he? I know she was a difficult woman, but everything I've learnt about Braid suggests that he was fond of her."

"But then…I know!" Another idea had suddenly struck David. "Suppose that Malcolm Braid killed Father Thomas. And Louise found out and was going to shop him."

Gawaine's gaze suddenly became intent, focused. As so often before, David could almost see the little wheels going round in his head. Then the look of concentration gradually faded. "Attractive, but it won't work," he said. "Malcolm Braid has no motive for killing Father Thomas."

"No motive that we know of."

"True. But remember that he has an alibi too. He's one of the people who were looking for Father Thomas after he disappeared. He couldn't be doing that *and* luring him away to get murdered."

"I suppose so," David conceded.

"And if he were guilty, far from shopping him, I'm sure Louise would have done her best to keep it all quiet."

Regretfully, David had to agree. "Then you think someone else might have murdered Louise? But who else would have any sort of stake in her death?"

Gawaine turned sideways so that he was facing David, briefly running a hand over the brass plaque on the back of the bench, which informed all and sundry that it was placed there in memory of H C Gordon, late captain of the Ellingwood Cricket Club.

"A relic of more peaceful days..." Gawaine murmured. Then he obviously made an effort to concentrate. "We thought that Dr Jerrold had no motive. But suppose, for the sake of argument, that Louise's infatuation with him was not in fact unrequited. Perhaps her flat over the surgery was their...er...love-nest."

"Oh, come on!" David exclaimed. "Having an affair with Louise when he was married to a hot – I mean, a more attractive woman like Amy?"

"No one knows what goes on inside someone else's marriage," Gawaine pointed out. "And Louise may have had attractions that were not visible on the surface."

"Good in bed, you mean?"

Gawaine winced. "Possibly. However, indulge me, my dear David. I am assuming – and I should be very much surprised if I'm wrong – that Louise was Dr Jerrold's patient."

David began to see where Gawaine was going. "Malcolm Braid told us that the doctor had given her some sleeping stuff," he said. "And if he was going to bed with his patient..."

"A very bad move, for his career as well as his marriage," Gawaine went on. "Now suppose further that Father Thomas had found out about this affair. The doctor, of course, was not one of his congregation, but Louise was, and so Father Thomas would have felt it his duty to put a stop to it."

"So Louise goes to Dr Jerrold, tells him that Father Thomas knows…" David said, excitement building up inside him.

"That gives him a very good motive for the murder," Gawaine agreed.

David contemplated the idea for a moment, then shook his head. "That still doesn't explain how he got Father Thomas to leave the vestry."

Gawaine's blue eyes were suddenly bleak. "Nothing easier. He goes into the vestry. 'Father Thomas, Mrs So-and-so is dying and she wants the last rites. You have to come right away.' That would work."

"You're right, it would," David said. "So what are we going to do about it?"

"I think we go to have a talk with the doctor."

As they approached the surgery again, David spotted Dr Jerrold as he emerged and tossed a bag into a car parked in the street outside. Gawaine intercepted him before he could get into the car.

"Excuse me," he said. "Dr Jerrold? Could I have a word with you?"

"Who the hell are you?" Dr Jerrold asked, clearly not in the best of moods.

David paid close attention to him for the first time. He was a smallish man, sandy-haired, with a weak, petulant mouth. David guessed that Amy wore the pants in that household, so maybe the threat of sacking Louise had been more serious than it seemed at first.

Gawaine introduced himself. "I'm looking into Father Thomas's death on behalf of the bishop," he said.

"That's nothing to do with me. I'm not religious."

"But Father Thomas's murder might have some connection with the death of Louise Braid."

"I've already spoken to the police about that." Dr Jerrold was getting more annoyed by the minute. "Louise was a silly, hysterical woman and if she chose to kill herself there's nothing I could do about it."

"Do you feel that the scene in the restaurant last Wednesday – "

"I'm not going to discuss that," Dr Jerrold interrupted. "It's personal, and none of your business. Now if you don't mind, I have house calls to make."

He shouldered Gawaine out of the way and got into the car. Gawaine stood back as he drove off.

"Nice bloke," David commented. "I wonder what Louise saw in him?"

Gawaine shrugged. "Love is blind, and all that, my dear David."

"You know, I could imagine him enjoying Louise's attention," David went on, watching the doctor's car as it drove out of sight. "All the cups of coffee, special biscuits, running his errands for him… Maybe he really had given her reason to think that he…well, that he had feelings for her."

"You know more about these things than I," Gawaine said. "In which case, Louise's dreams would have been truly shattered that night in the restaurant. Maybe it was a strong enough motive for suicide after all."

"So you don't think the doctor murdered her – and Father Thomas?"

"The jury is out, my dear David," Gawaine replied. "But there isn't a scrap of evidence that they had an affair, never mind that Father Thomas knew about it, so how could we possibly prove it? Besides, why would Dr Jerrold then murder his inamorata?"

"Because she guessed he was guilty, and he couldn't trust her to keep her mouth shut?"

Gawaine frowned. "Maybe. But she was still all over him in the restaurant on Wednesday, so he had no reason to mistrust her."

"Ah, but *after* the scene in the restaurant? Suppose Louise had told Jerrold that unless he kept her on – as his receptionist and his lover – she would spill the beans?"

"So possibly breaking up his marriage, if Amy was still insisting he get rid of Louise?" Gawaine briefly looked interested, than gave a slight shake of his head. "No, my dear David. If advertising fails you, you might be able to make a successful second career in writing sensational fiction. As I said, there's no evidence they were even having an affair, and plenty to suggest they weren't."

"Suicide, then?" David said. He wasn't sure which theory he liked better: Louise killing herself because of the prospect of losing her job, her flat, and the object of her affections, or said object murdering her to cover up his evil deeds.

Gawaine nodded reluctantly. "And we seem to be no further in finding out who really *did* kill Father Thomas."

Chapter Twenty

From battle and murder, and from sudden death, Good
Lord deliver us.

The Litany

On Saturday morning David was finishing his breakfast,
and Gawaine, looking agreeably ruffled in a blue silk
dressing gown, was slowly clawing his way back to
consciousness with the help of several cups of coffee,
when the telephone rang.

"Who's dead now?" David said.

Gawaine shuddered. "Don't."

He navigated carefully into the hall. Through the open
door David could hear his side of the conversation, consisting
of the occasional word interspersed with long periods of
silence. Finally Gawaine came back to the dining room and
sank gracefully into his chair again, groping for the coffee pot.

David grabbed it before Gawaine could knock it over,
and poured another cup for both of them. "Who was
that?" he asked.

"Christabel." Gawaine thrust a hand through ruffled
golden curls. "She wants a meeting."

"What on earth for?"

"I imagine, to give me my next set of orders. She's
caught up on all the gossip, about Louise Braid, and about

how the cross reappeared. She has now decided that Richard Coates is innocent, that Louise was murdered, and that it's my job to sort it all out. Under her guidance, naturally."

"Tell her to take a running jump."

Gawaine did not respond, merely sipped coffee with a helplessly fragile air. David knew very well that it wasn't in him to tell Christabel – or indeed anyone else – to take a running jump.

"So when do we leave?" he asked.

"An hour ago, according to Christabel. However, as things stand, as soon as we can get there." He pushed his coffee cup away. "I'm going to take a shower."

As David parked his car outside Christabel's house, the front door sprang open. Christabel appeared and stood there, clearly simmering, while he and Gawaine joined her.

"This is absolutely terrible!" she said, not bothering to respond to Gawaine's greeting. "We're all going to be murdered in our beds. What are you going to do about it?"

"I know it's frightfully unpleasant," Gawaine said. "But I don't think there's anything to be actually afraid of."

Christabel snorted and gestured them inside. David guessed that underneath her disagreeable manner, she was genuinely worried. He could understand that. Murders in English villages on TV were one thing; having them in your own back yard was quite another.

"You know, everything suggests that Louise Braid committed suicide," Gawaine said as Christabel led the way into her drawing room. David thought that he still didn't sound certain about that, and wondered if he was having second thoughts about Dr Jerrold as double murderer.

"Nonsense! Why would she?" Christabel retorted.

"The theory is that she was upset about the thing on Wednesday night," Gawaine replied. He took the chair Christabel indicated and refused her offer of coffee. "You did hear about that?"

"Oh, her stupid infatuation with Gregory Jerrold," Christabel said. "But that was all in her head. Surely not enough to kill herself over?"

"Men have died from time to time," Gawaine murmured in agreement, "and worms have eaten them, but not for love."

Christabel ignored that.

"Don't forget Louise was publicly humiliated," David said, repeating the arguments he had used on Gawaine the day before. "And if Amy Jerrold had her way, she would have lost her job and her flat."

"Oh, I suppose so," Christabel admitted with an irritated gesture. "Though I can't see Gregory sacking a perfectly efficient receptionist – and Louise *was* efficient, whatever else you say about her – no matter what Amy said."

"But did Louise think he would?" David asked.

"I'll speak again to DCI Ferris," Gawaine said, as Christabel's simmer seemed to be rising to a full rolling boil. "There should be more evidence in by now that might settle the thing one way or another."

"Hmm…" Christabel began to pace the room, stopping here and there to fiddle with an ornament. "You still don't seem to be any further on with finding out who killed

Father Thomas," she went on, changing tack. "It seems as if this Coates man must be innocent, since the cross turned up while he was in prison."

"I know," Gawaine said. "And that's the one good thing to have come out of the last couple of days. But the return of the cross, Louise's death...they don't seem to have anything to do with the original murder."

"Are you saying you're at a dead end?" Christabel asked.

"I'm afraid so."

Christabel let out an elaborate sigh, the sound of the long-suffering faced with impenetrable stupidity. "I should never have asked you to do this in the first place."

No, you shouldn't, David thought.

"I really think I shall have to call that extraordinary general meeting of the PCC," Christabel continued. "After the nine fifteen service tomorrow, in church. We can all get together and talk this out. Maybe *somebody* will have a few ideas."

"I wish you the best of luck," Gawaine said.

Christabel stared at him. "You will, of course, be there."

"I don't think so," David said, pre-empting Gawaine's response, which would, he guessed, have been weak-kneed agreement.

Christabel flashed him a glare, consigning him to outer darkness. "You *will* co-operate," she told Gawaine. "The PCC are ready to advertise for our new vicar, and how can we do that, with the murder hanging over us?"

Gawaine, who was contemplating his fingernails, murmured something inaudible, which to David's annoyance sounded like assent.

"At least we can make sure that we get someone suitable," Christabel went on. "No more of this Anglo-Catholic nonsense. Crossing and genuflecting, fasting on Fridays, and filling the church with candles and incense…"

Gawaine's head suddenly came up; he was alert, intent. David froze; he had seen that look before. The silence seemed to stretch out for centuries.

"*Now* what's the matter?" Christabel asked at last. "Are you – ?"

"My dear Christabel," Gawaine interrupted, all affectation now, "I'm sure the bishop will find you a perfectly suitable priest for St Paul's. But now we have to go. I shall be delighted to see you tomorrow at the meeting."

"Are you out of your mind?" David asked as they got back into his car. "Why on earth would you agree to turn up and be grilled by Christabel and her cronies?"

Gawaine turned towards him, but his eyes were blank, inward-looking. "Being grilled is not what I have in mind."

David's mind raced, putting together what he had heard at Christabel's, and finding no rational explanation, only remembering the times he had seen Gawaine like this before.

"You know, don't you?" he asked, half excited, half appalled at the thought of what his friend would have to go through in the next twenty-four hours.

Gawaine nodded. "I'm almost sure. I just need to see Katie Rook."

"Who?"

"Katie Rook. The acolyte – the girl who saw Father Thomas in the vestry. I need to ask her one question."

David put the car into gear and drove slowly away from Christabel's house. "Do you know where she lives?"

"No, but we can look them up in the phone book at the Farrier's Arms."

Looking things up online, as David knew very well, was never Gawaine's first thought, but given that the pub was only a couple of minutes away, going there would probably be quicker.

David pulled into the car park. "Wait here," he said. "I'll go in through the passage. We should probably avoid Seff at this stage."

Gawaine replied with only an abstracted mutter. He was obviously thinking deeply. Leaving him to it, David wondered again what had sparked this off. Something Christabel had said? Something Gawaine had seen in her house?

It would have to be pretty startling to bring this on, David thought. *And to make Gawaine ready to face Christabel and her lot tomorrow.*

He slid quickly through the back door of the pub and down the passage to where the phone book still sat on its shelf. There was only one Rook in Ellingwood; David scribbled the address on the back of his hand and headed out into the car park again.

Rounding the corner of the building, he spotted a police car drive past the car park entrance, then halt and reverse until it turned in and parked beside his own car. DCI Ferris got out and tapped on David's car window.

David was close enough to see Gawaine look up, startled, and emerge to face the DCI.

"I'm glad I spotted you," Ferris said as David walked up, sticking his hands in his pockets to hide the Rooks' address. "I wanted to tell you that we've released Richard Coates." He was sounding a lot friendlier than the last time David had met him – perhaps because Gawaine had been proved right. "We've given him strict instructions not to leave the area, but I think we'll have to accept his story. The cross turning up like that, and then Louise Braid…"

"Are you treating Louise Braid's death as murder?" David asked, after a pause in which it became quite obvious that Gawaine's mind was still elsewhere.

Ferris paused before replying. "I reckon she killed herself," he said at last. "But as I said yesterday, I'm going to make damn' sure."

"Did she leave a note?" David asked.

Once again Ferris hesitated, as if he was reluctant to disgorge the information. Yet David guessed that he felt a sense of obligation to Gawaine and maybe – though he would never have admitted it – a need for guidance.

"Yes, there was a note," Ferris replied. "It said, 'It's all too much. I can't bear it.' I compared the handwriting with some notes in her office, and it looks the same, but I've got an expert checking it."

Gawaine blinked, as if he had returned from some distant galaxy. David realised that some part of him had been listening all along. "Fingerprints?" he asked.

"Just hers on the note," Ferris said. "In fact the only fingerprints in the bedroom were hers, except for her brother's, on the bin liner."

"So he could have tied the bag on her," David said.

"He could," Ferris grunted. "But his prints were on top of his sister's, which tallies with his story that he found her and took the bag off."

"But anyone else…" Gawaine began. He spoke slowly and dreamily, as if he was following a thread that only he could see. "Anyone else, knowing she would have taken her sleeping stuff, could have come in, wearing gloves, tied the bag on her head, dabbed her own prints all over it, and then left her…" His voice trailed off and he shuddered.

"Quite possible," DCI Ferris said heavily. "But then you need to find someone who had knowledge of her pills, and access to the flat. Which brings it down to Malcolm Braid or Dr Jerrold."

"Or Mrs Jerrold," David said.

Ferris nodded. "Or Mrs Jerrold. I think I shall have to have words with the doctor and his wife."

Gawaine gave himself a little shake, as if he was casting off unwelcome thoughts. "I'm sure you know your own business best, Chief Inspector," he said, sounding suddenly more aware, his tones crisp. "But I have one recommendation. Tomorrow, after the morning service at St Paul's, I shall be making a report to the PCC. If you could be there, I think you would find it interesting."

David stared at him. *I'd no idea he was that far along… not ready to hand over to the police!*

Ferris was staring, too, the old unfriendliness back in his expression. "If you have any information…"

"Oh, no, Chief Inspector, I haven't. Not as such. But by tomorrow I hope to have. Do join us at St Paul's," he added, as if he was inviting Ferris for tea on the lawn.

"Maybe I will, at that," the DCI said.

He got back into his car and the sergeant drove off. David was about to do the same when Gawaine touched him on the arm. "Give him a moment. I don't want him thinking that it might be useful to follow us."

He settled into the passenger seat while David punched the Rooks' postcode into his satnav. By the time he was ready, and the annoyingly prissy voice had told him to turn left out of the car park, the police car was long gone.

The Rooks' house was at the far end of the village, on the edge of the modern development. Its aggressive red brick was softened by a vine growing up the front and two white-painted half barrels standing on either side of the door, planted with chrysanthemums and Michaelmas daisies.

David drew up outside the front gate. Gawaine gave him a tense look before getting out of the car and heading up the path. David followed, feeling this might be the time to say, "This is it', or 'Once more unto the breach', or even, 'Geronimo!' but he ended by saying nothing.

The plump, dark-haired woman they had spoken to in the church hall car park answered the doorbell, and gave a wide smile, obviously recognising Gawaine. "Oh, it's you! Come in. Is there anything I can do for you?"

"I'd like a word with Katie," Gawaine replied, "if that's all right with you."

Mrs Rook halted in the hall with one hand stretched out to push a door open. "She was really upset about Father Thomas," she said. "You will be careful, won't you?"

Gawaine nodded. "One question. I promise."

With a sigh of relief Mrs Rook opened the door and led the way into an untidy sitting-room. Two little boys were playing some sort of game with sofa cushions all over the floor. An older girl was sitting on one of the cushions, her back against the wall, with a ginger cat on her lap and her nose in a book.

"Katie," her mother said, "this is Mr St Clair, who is helping the police find out about what happened to Father Thomas. He'd like to ask you something."

The girl sprang to her feet, scattering the book and the cat. David thought she looked about twelve, small and thin with a tangle of dark hair. She was wearing cut-off jeans and a baggy T-shirt with a huge leopard face on the front.

"I'll help if I can," she said. "But I told everything to the police."

Gawaine nodded. The cat was weaving around his feet, purring, obviously recognizing a kindred spirit.

"Katie," Gawaine began, "you said that when you went into the vestry to fetch the taper, Father Thomas had his back to you."

"That's right," Katie replied. "I was scared he would tell me off, but he didn't see me."

"Can you remember what he was doing?"

Katie nodded eagerly. "Oh, yes," she said. "He was putting on his amice."

Chapter Twenty-one

For now is the ax put to the root of the tree, so that every tree that bringeth not forth good fruit is hewn down, and cast into the fire.

A Commination

In the next twenty-four hours, David asked a multitude of questions, ranging from, "What's an amice?" to "Whodunit?" but he did not receive a reply. Gawaine spent most of his time in his sitting room, now staring into space, now making meticulous notes on his pad. David struggled with frustration, even though he had been through this before. Gawaine hated so much the moment when he had to explain, that he could not be expected to do it more than once.

All that Gawaine said, in the car on the way to St Paul's the next morning, was, "I know how. I know who. What I don't know is why."

A stiff breeze was blowing, whirling the leaves from the trees and slapping the first few drops of rain against David's windscreen as he pulled into the church hall car park. The hall doors were open, and a few stragglers were making their way across the road. David noticed that a police car was parked among the rest, and drew Gawaine's attention to it.

"Ferris is here."

"Good."

Gawaine's voice was colourless. He looked white and strained, and David thought he could discern a slight tremor in his hands.

Almost as soon as David had switched off the engine, Christabel was swooping down on them.

"There you are! We're meeting in the church." As David and Gawaine got out of the car, she added, "Was it you who told the police about this?"

"Indeed it was, my dear Christabel." Now Gawaine's affectations were firmly in place, his disquiet carefully concealed. "We may find that before this is over, we have need of the attentions of DCI Ferris."

Christabel merely snorted, and led the way over the road to the church.

By this time the bulk of the congregation had left. George Marshall and Malcolm Braid were arranging chairs into a circle in the wide space between the pews and the back wall of the church. Several other people – the members of the PCC, David supposed – were milling around with a vaguely disgruntled air, as though they were worried about a delayed Sunday lunch. David spotted the Hartleys, Andrew Danby, Charles Cottesmore, John Bretton poring over a clip-board, and a number of others he didn't recognise.

David also noticed DCI Ferris and his sergeant, sitting at the end of one of the back pews, half turned towards the gathering. The sergeant had his notebook out.

Then a flicker of movement drew his gaze further up the church, a flash of glossy chestnut hair and a bright turquoise jacket, vanishing behind a pillar. He touched Gawaine's arm. "Seff is here."

"Ah, you spotted her, my dear David," Gawaine murmured. "And she has Leah Koroma with her. I wonder if that was entirely wise."

Given what was about to happen, David thought it was entirely crazy. He wondered briefly how Seff had found out about the meeting, then dismissed the thought. Sooner or later Seff found out about everything.

"Is she out of her mind?" he whispered, seeing the two women settle themselves in a pew about half way up the church. "Bringing Leah here..."

Gawaine gave him a bright, intent look. "On reflection, my dear David, and given the circumstances, perhaps Leah has more right than most people to be here."

By this time the chairs were in place and people were finding seats.

"Sit!" Christabel commanded, gesturing to a pair of unoccupied chairs.

"Woof!" David muttered, seating himself beside Gawaine.

John Bretton took a seat opposite, consulted his clip-board, then looked up to fix Gawaine with a cold stare.

"We have a few questions for you," he stated. "First of all – "

"No," Gawaine interrupted.

Bretton glared. "I *beg* your pardon?"

David hid a grin. He always enjoyed the moments when Gawaine – normally so amenable that the unwary mistook it for weakness – sat up and showed teeth.

Bretton's glare might have worked on recalcitrant schoolboys, but on this occasion it had no effect at all on Gawaine. "No," he repeated. "That's not why I'm here. Instead, I propose to tell you exactly what has been happening in this village, and exactly what happened to Father Thomas."

Shocked exclamations from his audience. One of them let out a guffaw: a rotund man in shabby tweeds, with puffy red cheeks and a bristling moustache. "Really? You mean we're like the suspects gathered in the library, and Poirot or some such comes along and says, 'The murderer is in this room'?"

"Indeed, Colonel Sutton," Gawaine said with controlled distaste. "If you wish to be melodramatic, the murderer is in this church."

More shocked gasps. Beryl Hartley had her hand pressed to her mouth, and Christabel looked as if she was working up for some serious pearl-clutching.

"You can't know that!" she exclaimed.

Gawaine made no response, and it was Charles Cottesmore who spoke. "I think we'd better listen."

David glanced around as the PCC members settled themselves again. Several of them looked shocked, others anxious or merely interested. No one had a guilty look; whoever the murderer was, he had the strength to hide what he surely must be feeling.

Gawaine paused for a moment, looking down at his note-pad, then raised his head again and faced his audience. "The whole problem of Father Thomas's murder," he began, "boils down to the question of who or what made him leave the vestry at such a crucial time, without even taking a moment to tell someone that he was going."

"We know *that*," Bretton said.

Gawaine ignored the interruption. "I found two suspects with the capacity to do that," he went on. "Richard Coates, with news of an accident to their sister, or Dr Jerrold, asking for help with a dying patient."

Someone exclaimed, "Dr Jerrold?" in a soft, disbelieving voice.

"However," Gawaine said, "even in those instances, it would be unlikely for Father Thomas not to take a few seconds to tell someone else what he needed to do. Yet he did not do so. Instead, he sent a text to Malcolm Braid, apologising and asking him to take the evening service. Still, you will note, giving no explanation for where he was going or why."

The bristly-moustached man – Colonel Sutton – shifted in his seat. "Look, we've all been over this, time and again, in our own minds. Where is all this leading?"

Gawaine blinked at him. "To the truth. And now I have a confession to make, because I have had two pieces of information from the very early stages of this inquiry, and I failed to put them together until yesterday." He closed his eyes briefly, as if struck by a sudden pain. "I find it hard to forgive myself for that."

"What information, for goodness' sake?" Christabel asked.

Gawaine looked up again. "You gave me the first yourself, Christabel," he replied. "That Father Thomas was a strict Anglo-Catholic. You mentioned that again yesterday, referring to how he would fast on Fridays, and that was what made me realise what I'd been missing."

Christabel stared, uncomprehending, while the other members of the PCC exchanged uneasy glances.

"The second piece of information," Gawaine went on, "came from DCI Ferris, that Father Thomas's stomach contents showed that he had eaten a meal about an hour before he was killed. Eggs on toast for breakfast was his guess." Gawaine paused and let his glance travel around the circle. "But a strict Anglo-Catholic priest fasts at other times besides Fridays. He fasts before he takes Communion. And there was no earlier service. Therefore the eggs on toast were not his breakfast, but his supper of the night before. Father Thomas was not killed on the Sunday morning, but on the previous Saturday evening."

David felt a jolt as if he had been kicked in the stomach. His whole view of the case was crumbling away like a bombed out building, and he had no idea how Gawaine proposed to rebuild it.

He expected an outcry from Gawaine's listeners, but apart from a few gasps of shock they mostly received the revelation in stunned silence.

"But my daughter saw him in the vestry!" A hatchet-faced individual David had not seen before sprang to his feet from across the circle. "Are you calling Katie a liar?"

"Mr Rook." Gawaine inclined his head briefly. "No, I'm convinced that Katie told the truth about what she saw. And that leads us to the question: what exactly did Katie Rook see? I'll come back to that in a moment."

He paused while the outraged Mr Rook took his seat again, somewhat mollified. David still didn't see where Gawaine was going. How could a man be killed on the Saturday night and turn up in the vestry on the Sunday morning?

There were no more interruptions from the Council members. They were all intent now, their gaze fixed on Gawaine. By now, David knew, someone must be squirming, but whoever he was, he gave no outward sign.

"The murderer killed his victim on the Saturday night," Gawaine went on. "Later, I think I can safely assume, he put the body in his car and drove up to the North Downs, where he left it in a convenient thicket, having removed Father Thomas's mobile phone, his keys and his pectoral cross. The police thought he did that to delay identification, but then he left the body still wearing its cassock and clerical collar, which shows that hiding its identity was not a priority. I'm sure that he hoped the body would never be found, but failing that, he knew that other methods – dental records, DNA – would have proved fairly quickly who it was."

He paused to take a deep breath. David gave him a quick glance; he knew what this must be costing his friend, though outwardly Gawaine was in control.

"But then how – ?" Christabel began.

Charles Cottesmore reached out to put a hand on her arm, and gave her a firm shake of the head. To David's astonishment, Christabel shut up.

"Either before or after his trip to the North Downs," Gawaine went on, "and whether it was before or after is immaterial, the murderer put on Father Thomas's cloak and rode his bicycle back through the village to the vicarage."

"We saw him!" Christabel exclaimed. "We'd been for dinner at the Farrier's Arms, and we saw him on our way back!"

Gawaine nodded to her. "I remember you told me that. And that it was a nasty night," he said. "A stroke of luck for the murderer, since it allowed him to wear the cloak with its hood up, and meant no one who saw him would want to stop and chat, or even look at him very closely. You saw a man wearing Father Thomas's cloak, riding Father Thomas's bicycle, and you naturally assumed that he was Father Thomas."

"We saw him too, Marjorie and I," Andrew Danby said. "We'd just come out of the pub, and he went sailing past on the other side of the green."

"At the vicarage," Gawaine continued, "the murderer, who had of course taken Father Thomas's keys, put the bicycle away in the garage and the cloak in its proper place in the coat cupboard. He then left and made his way home, I'm guessing by footpaths rather than the main streets."

Could that have been John Bretton? David wondered, eyeing the man suspiciously. He would have had the easiest escape route, down the footpath that led from Church Lane to the school. Bretton was drumming his fingers on his clipboard, but that looked like ordinary impatience rather than nervousness fuelled by guilt.

Gawaine consulted his notes once again, and continued. "Now we come to the Sunday morning. The murderer needs to create evidence that Father Thomas was still alive. So – "

"But Katie *saw* him!" Rook protested again. "You're not telling me she made a mistake, not with his height and that head of blazing red hair."

"Give me time," Gawaine assured him. Glancing around the rest of the circle, he went on, "You see that we have now eliminated the two original suspects, Richard Coates and Dr Jerrold. Neither of them were members of this church, and therefore they wouldn't have the knowledge to do what the murderer did. Nor, incidentally, would Frank Reed."

"But what *did* the murderer do?" Beryl Hartley asked, in an agony of impatience.

"He knew that George Marshall would have unbolted the outer door to the priest's vestry by ten to nine," Gawaine replied. "He therefore let himself in, and choosing his moment carefully, he moved the taper from the servers' vestry into the priest's vestry, knowing that at some point one of the servers would have to come in and retrieve it. He then put on part of the priest's vestments, and waited."

"Waited for the server to come in and fetch the taper!" David said.

"Exactly."

"But just a minute," George Marshall put in. "Okay, I can see how he arranged it so someone would see he was there. But I can't understand how anyone here could be mistaken for Father Thomas. He was pretty distinctive."

"His *hair* was pretty distinctive," Gawaine agreed. "But if the murderer could cover up his head... That's why I went to see Katie Rook yesterday and asked her what Father Thomas was doing when she saw him. And she told me that he was putting on his amice."

George Marshall let out a sudden exclamation of understanding, though the rest of the PCC remained mystified.

"An amice, for those who aren't familiar with it," Gawaine went on, with a glance at DCI Ferris, still in his pew, "is part of the priest's vestments. It's a piece of fabric that is put on initially like a hood, fastened, and then slides down to form a collar. If Katie caught the murderer in the act of putting it on, she wouldn't have been able to see his hair, because the fabric of the amice would be covering it."

"But – " George Marshall began.

Gawaine lifted a hand to silence him. "That only leaves the one other salient characteristic of Father Thomas," he continued, at his most pedantic. "His height. There is no way in which a murderer could simulate Father Thomas's height. And so that eliminates many of our possible suspects. You yourself, Mr Marshall, Mr Hartley, Colonel Sutton, Mr Danby…you are all too short to have been mistaken for him. Richard Coates and Frank Reed have the height, but they are both much broader in the shoulders, and in any case they have been eliminated for other reasons. That only leaves one possibility." Gawaine turned his head until his gaze rested on Malcolm Braid.

"Mr Braid," he asked, "why did you kill your priest?"

Chapter Twenty-two

We acknowledge and bewail our manifold sins and wickedness, which we from time to time most grievously have committed.

A General Confession

Malcolm Braid gave Gawaine a cold stare from protuberant blue eyes. "I've never heard such a load of nonsense," he said.

"Are you denying this?" John Bretton snapped out the words.

"Of course I'm denying it!"

David could sense hostility as well as confusion coming from the members of the PCC. He realised that some of them at least had been convinced by Gawaine's explanation. And as Gawaine had predicted, they would throw Braid to the wolves if they thought he had committed a murder.

Gawaine remained silent; he looked tired and unhappy, and still on edge, as if he knew there was still a long way to go before it was all over.

"Malcolm, maybe if you could tell us what you were doing on that Saturday night..." Charles Cottesmore suggested, sounding reasonable.

"I don't have to tell you anything!" Braid responded.

With a venomous glance at Gawaine, he added, "There is such a thing as slander."

Before Gawaine could reply, DCI Ferris stood up and tramped across to stand behind Braid's chair. "I've heard enough, sir, to ask you to come to the station for questioning."

Braid simply clamped his mouth shut, looking furious.

"We need a warrant to search Mr Braid's property," Ferris went on, turning to his sergeant. "And his car. If he is guilty, there'll be traces."

David thought that he saw Malcolm Braid tense, as if with the sudden realisation that refusing to speak, or flinging around accusations of slander, wouldn't do him any good in the long run. But he still said nothing.

A flicker of movement further up the church distracted David for a moment. He saw that Leah Koroma had risen to her feet. Seff reached out and tugged her arm, whispering something. After a moment, Leah subsided into the pew again.

"If you don't mind, sir…" said Ferris.

Braid still refused to move or speak.

"Malcolm, an innocent man was arrested," Charles Cottesmore said, his voice level but determined. "And we've all been giving each other suspicious looks, ever since Father Thomas's body was found. If you're innocent, then answer the Chief Inspector's questions and have done with it. But if you are guilty…good God, man, what's the point of going on denying it?"

Malcolm Braid met his gaze stonily for a moment. Then his shoulders sagged and he let out a long sigh. "Have it your own way," he said wearily. "I'll be glad to have it over with." Turning to Gawaine, he added, "Years ago they would have burned you at the stake. You had it all right, except for a few details."

"Then tell us why," Gawaine said quietly.

Malcolm Braid sat with his hands clasped between his knees and his head bowed. For a moment he said nothing, and DCI Ferris, with a dubious glance at Gawaine, retreated to his pew again and sat beside his sergeant.

"I wasn't always Malcolm Braid," he admitted at last. "When I was born, my parents named me Marie."

A stunned silence greeted Braid's revelation, broken after a few moments by Henry Hartley. "You were a *girl*?"

Christabel's voice rose almost to a shriek. "You changed your sex?"

To begin with, David couldn't see what all the fuss was about. *Have they never come across a transgender person before?* Then he realised that in the safe, respectable community of Ellingwood, particularly among the congregation of St Paul's, perhaps they never had. He could see that Ellingwood might not be the most friendly place in the world for anyone who didn't fit their definition of 'normal'. *But would it be bad enough to murder..?*

Then the horrified expressions that had greeted Braid's confession began to show David how bad it might have been. Colonel Sutton looked outraged, purplish colour mounting in his cheeks, while Christabel had a pinched expression as if there was a bad smell under her nose.

"I didn't *change* anything," Braid responded, still staring at the floor. "I was always a man. I was just born in the wrong body. Eventually I had the chance to put that right, and live the life that I was meant to live."

"It must have been very difficult for you," Charles Cottesmore said quietly.

Braid nodded. "School was a nightmare. I didn't look right, I didn't behave right, and you know what kids can be like… University wasn't so bad, and for a while I tried to live as a woman. I even got married." He let out a harsh puff of laughter. "That was a disaster. My husband was delighted to give me a divorce, and then I had the surgery. After that, everything changed, but I had to leave the old life behind me, and find a place to live where no one knew me from before."

"That's all well and good," Christabel said, "and I'm sure I'm sorry if you had a hard time, but did you have to come *here*? Wouldn't you have been happier in London, along with others of your kind?"

Braid flashed her a sidelong glance, anger in his eyes. "I don't have a *kind*," he snapped. "All I ever wanted was to be an ordinary man, leading an ordinary life, in an ordinary place."

Christabel lapsed into an affronted silence, her lips pressed tightly together.

"Louise always stood by me," Malcolm Braid went on. "She was already working for Dr Jerrold, and she told me that there was an opening at the solicitors'. But she insisted that I didn't tell anyone about my background."

David could understand that. Life would have been tough for Louise Braid if her brother had been ostracised.

"So what happened?" Gawaine asked. His expression was full of pained compassion, and David could tell how much effort it took for him to ask the question. "I take it Father Thomas found out?"

For the first time, Malcolm Braid raised his head and met Gawaine's gaze. "It started with the commentary on Luke's Gospel," he said. "The one you returned to me. Father Thomas borrowed it from me because most of his books were still in transit somewhere between here and Sierra Leone. But I'd forgotten that I'd used a photograph to mark a page in it…a photograph of me and Louise, while I was still in a woman's body. And Father Thomas found it."

"But wait a minute," David said. "Why was that a problem? You could have said that it was another sister in the photograph – maybe one living in Australia, or anywhere a long way off. How did Father Thomas know it was you?"

"Because of this." Malcolm Braid shrugged off his jacket and unfastened the cuff of his left shirt sleeve. Pulling up the sleeve, he revealed a jagged white scar, running up his forearm from his wrist to his elbow. "One of the kids at school thought it would be fun to throw me through a plate glass window," he said. "Father Thomas had seen the scar when I rolled my sleeves up to help him unclog a drain at the vicarage. And it showed in the photograph. Father Thomas wasn't stupid. He knew what it meant. He knew that two separate people couldn't have the exact same scar in the exact same place."

"And that's why he came to see you on that Saturday night," Gawaine said.

"Yes. He wasn't angry. In fact, he was quite sympathetic. But he made it quite clear that things couldn't go on as they were. He said that he would go on giving me Communion provided that I went on living celibate. But he couldn't go on working with me as lay reader."

"Quite right, too," John Bretton muttered.

"I begged him to reconsider, or at least to give me some time," Braid said. "After all, I was due to preach the following morning. If I hadn't done that, the gossip would have started. And sooner or later it would all have come out."

"And then..?" Gawaine prompted delicately.

"We argued about it for some time. I tried to tell Father Thomas what it would mean to me. I'd have lost my work for the church, and probably my job as well. The other two partners are father and son, and the old man is a stickler for convention. Besides, most of my clients live in Ellingwood or the country round about, and a good half of them are members of this congregation. How many of them would I have managed to keep? And there was Louise... She would have been devastated to have it all made public. How many friends would she have had left?"

"There would have been some," Beryl Hartley said.

Braid shook his head. "We both remembered what we did – what *we* did," he repeated fiercely, staring around at the members of the PCC, "to Chantal Dupont. Louise couldn't have borne it if it had happened to us...she couldn't bear it."

"So that's why she killed herself!" David exclaimed.

Gawaine raised a hand to silence him. "Let's have that in its proper place," he said. "Go on, Mr Braid."

Braid took in a long breath, and started again. "Whatever I said, Father Thomas wouldn't budge. He was so sure he was right – but I saw him as summing up all the people who had sneered at me and attacked me over the years. He was going to take away everything I'd

221

ever worked for. And I panicked. When he was leaving, I grabbed a statuette that stands in my hall." He screwed his eyes shut for a moment as if he was trying to wipe out the memory. "And for a second everything went black. I hit him with the statue, but I hardly realised I was doing it.

"As soon as he was dead, I wanted to turn time back so it hadn't happened. But I knew that all I could do was try to arrange things so I wouldn't be blamed for it. Louise had seen him when he arrived, and for all I knew other people too, so I couldn't pretend that he had never been there."

"So what did you do?"

David started at the harsh sound of DCI Ferris's voice from outside the circle. He had risen from his pew and taken a couple of steps towards Braid. His sergeant was scribbling frantically in the notebook.

Braid still spoke to Gawaine. "First of all I put the body into the boot of my car. That was easy, because my garage is attached, and there was no risk of being seen. Then I cleaned everything up. By then it was dark, and I'd had the idea of riding Father Thomas's bike back to the vicarage, to make it seem as if he'd left. I tried to time it for when people would be leaving the Farrier's Arms, so that I'd be seen. And while I was doing all that, I had the idea of making it seem as if Father Thomas had been alive on the Sunday morning."

"Manipulating *my child*," Rook said, sounding dangerous.

Braid shrugged helplessly. "I'm sorry. I didn't know it would be Katie."

"Just get on with it," Ferris said.

222

Braid turned back to Gawaine. "You made one mistake there," he continued. "That night, before I left the bike and the cloak at the vicarage, I used Father Thomas's keys to let myself into the church, through the south door. I took my own cassock and the taper from the servers' vestry and hid them in the priest's vestry, so George wouldn't see them when he came to unbolt the door and get out the silver. So the following morning I didn't have to risk being seen in the servers' vestry."

Gawaine nodded. "I stand corrected. Go on."

"I made my way home by the footpaths through the woods, and in the early hours I drove up onto the Downs and hid the body. I took his phone, because I'd planned how I was going to use it, and his cross, because...well, because I couldn't just leave it there. Then I drove home.

"The following morning, it happened just as you said. I put the taper out in plain sight, and as soon as Katie had picked it up I took off the vestments and went down the path into the vicarage garden. I'd already put the text to myself into Father Thomas's phone, so all I had to do was send it. Then I came back up the path, mingled with the rest of the congregation, and helped to look for Father Thomas when George realised he was missing."

Somebody in the circle let out a long sigh. "Incredible."

Gawaine let the silence drag on for a few moments. He looked tense, wound up like a coil of wire, and white with exhaustion.

David touched him on the arm. "Leave it to Ferris now."

Gawaine turned his head to look at him, his blue eyes focused elsewhere. "No," he murmured. "We're not finished yet." To Braid, he added, "Tell us about Louise."

Braid flinched; his gaze went wildly from Gawaine to Ferris and back again. "I swear I didn't kill her!"

"We know that," Ferris said, and added to Gawaine, "Forensics came up with their report. Louise Braid had taken three times the normal dose of her sleeping pills. And our expert passed the note as genuine. It was suicide, all right."

"But something precipitated her death," Gawaine said. "I thought at the time that the incident with the Jerrolds was a weak motive for suicide, though I accepted it for want of a better. But it was more than that, wasn't it?"

Braid nodded. "She came home with me on Wednesday night and had a good cry, and I thought that would be the end of it. I told her that Jerrold would never sack her, and she seemed to accept that. She seemed more cheerful the next morning, and told me that while I was at work she meant to give my house a good turn-out." His mouth quirked. "She always thinks – thought – that I live in squalor if I just leave a dirty cup in the sink. So I went off to work, thinking the whole thing with the Jerrolds had blown over."

"But when you came home…" Gawaine murmured.

"She was in hysterics. She had decided to sort through my wardrobe and send some clothes to the dry cleaner's, and she found the cross."

Gawaine suddenly sat straighter and let out a long sigh. "Now I see…"

"When I hid Father Thomas's body," Malcolm Braid went on, "I took his phone and the cross, like I told you. I used his phone to send the text, then later I smashed it and dumped it in a pond, but I couldn't bring myself to get

224

rid of the cross. It was – well, it was a *cross*. It stayed in the pocket of the old anorak I'd worn when I transported the body. And that's where Louise found it."

"And realised what it meant?" Gawaine queried.

"Yes. It was that same day that the piece about the cross appeared in the paper, about what it meant to Father Thomas and his fiancée. I think without that I might have made up some sort of story to satisfy Louise, but as it was... She knew I'd killed Father Thomas. She was terrified it would all be found out, and she couldn't bear it. She screamed at me, "I don't want to be another Chantal!" She went home, and the next thing I knew, she was dead."

"And you returned the cross?" David asked.

"I knew the time had come to get rid of it, and I wanted Leah Koroma to have it. I thought it would be safe enough to drop it off in the Farrier's Arms. So I went for a drink that night. The bar was packed, and no one noticed when I put the package on the shelf by the phone."

"Good enough," Ferris said. "Sergeant."

He jerked his head towards Braid, who stood up to face the sergeant as he stepped up, and remained stone-faced as he began to speak. "Malcolm Braid, I'm arresting you for the murder of Thomas Coates…"

David tuned out the remainder of the familiar words, as the members of the PCC started to rise to their feet, shifting chairs and shuffling awkwardly about, as if no one quite knew how to bring the meeting to an end. No one seemed inclined to talk to Gawaine, who was sitting quite still, his gaze fixed on his clasped hands. His notepad had slid disregarded to the floor.

While he knew that they needed to get out of there, David was distracted by the sight of Leah approaching down the side aisle to the south door, with Seff close beside her. She stood, tears silently spilling down her face until the sergeant led Braid out to the waiting police car.

At the door Braid glanced up at her and muttered, "I'm sorry."

Leah still said nothing, only fixing huge dark eyes upon him until the sergeant gave him a shove and he stumbled through the door.

Ferris followed them, then paused in front of Leah. "You'll get the cross back, Miss, but it might be some time," he told her. "If you leave the country, let us have an address where we can get in touch with you."

Leah nodded. "I'm going to stay with Susan Cox for a while," she said in a husky voice. "You know where to find her?"

"I do." The DCI stuck out a hand, and after a moment Leah shook it. "Goodbye, Miss."

David turned back to Gawaine, who had still not moved, and rested a hand briefly on his shoulder. "We should go," he said.

Gawaine looked up at him, his expression distraught. "I should have known…" he murmured.

"What?" David couldn't understand his distress. "You did know. You worked it all out. Braid would have got away with it, if it wasn't for you."

"But I was too late." Gawaine's voice was quiet, every word forced out. "I had the information almost from the beginning, but I didn't see it. If I had, Louise Braid would still be alive."

"You can't say that!" David protested.

"Oh, but I can. If I had pulled all this together before Wednesday, that scene in the restaurant would never have happened. Louise wouldn't have *been* in the restaurant."

"But she would still have had to face up to her brother being a murderer," David pointed out. "And everyone would have found out that he's transgender. Who knows what she would have done then?"

"It would have been different. She would have had friends to support her…"

"She didn't *have* friends. And if this whole place wasn't so quick to pass judgement, the murder would never have happened. Braid should never have been driven to it. Aren't your lot supposed to believe something about compassion?"

"Judge not, that ye be not judged," Gawaine murmured, looking no less distressed.

"Besides," David went on, "do you think Ferris would have listened to your theory while he still had his case against Richard Coates sewn up so nice and neatly? He would never have taken you seriously until after Braid returned the cross."

Gawaine blinked unhappily. "You may have a point there."

"Come on," David said, standing up. "We're out of here."

Gawaine rose, too, but as David began steering him toward the south door, they were intercepted by George Marshall.

"Well done," he said. "At least we can stop looking at each other now, thinking *Was it you*?"

Gawaine nodded mutely and went on by, but before he reached the doors he was stopped again, this time by Leah, who reached out to take his hands.

"Thank you," she said.

Gawaine managed to meet her gaze, but David could see the tension thrilling through him. "It was nothing," he said.

Leah would have said more, but Seff touched her on her arm and gave a tiny shake of her head. She released Gawaine, who murmured a goodbye and walked out into the rain.

Epilogue

That it may please thee to bring into the way of truth all such as have erred, and are deceived...

The Litany

David Powers had just put on a pot of coffee, and was checking his phone for local takeaways, when the doorbell rang. Opening the door, he found Seff Brown on the step, her gleaming black Mini just visible in the darkness of the drive.

Oh, for crying out loud, what does she want?

David suppressed his first unchivalrous reaction and stepped back so that Seff could enter. "I thought you would have gone home by now," he said.

Seff shook her head. "I sent my story in, then I had lunch with Leah and drove her over to Guildford to Susan Cox," she explained.

"Is she okay?" David asked.

Seff gave him an exasperated look. "I'd expect you to know how it feels, to have your fiancée murdered," she said. "Though I suppose Leah was never accused of having done it. No, she's not okay," she added in reply to David's question, "but she's better for knowing the truth. She has Gawaine to thank for that."

So had I, David thought. Aloud, he said, "Do you want coffee?"

"Goodness, David, you're being very hospitable," Seff replied. "Are you sure you're feeling all right?"

Ignoring that with difficulty, David led the way into the kitchen, where the coffee percolator was making the appropriate gurgling noises.

"I came because I wanted to check that Gawaine is okay," Seff said, sitting at the kitchen table. "Where is he?"

"Gone to bed, with a sleeping pill and a couple of cats," David replied. "He was in a bit of a state. He can't stop blaming himself for Louise Braid's death."

"That's ridiculous," Seff said.

David was surprised to find that for once he was in agreement with her. He set milk and sugar on the table, poured two mugs of coffee, and took a seat opposite her. Taking in her glossy chestnut hair and wide hazel eyes, he felt a twinge of regret that such an attractive person should also be the most annoying woman in the world.

"Louise would never have coped with finding out that her brother murdered Father Thomas," Seff continued. "Whenever it came out. Especially given the reason for the murder. It would have shattered her life in the village."

David nodded. "They're a judgmental lot in Ellingwood."

"Yes, some of them should have trouble sleeping tonight. Though some won't; I expect Gawaine's Christabel still thinks she's in the right. I'm surprised Gawaine didn't tell her to shove off ages ago."

David stared at her. "Gawaine doesn't tell anyone to shove off, as you should know very well."

"Because he has never told me to shove off?" Seff grinned. "But he likes me. I'm sorry if that bothers you."

"Bother me? Why should it?" David clamped down firmly on the rising irritation that was all too familiar when dealing with Seff.

"I'm pretty sure he doesn't like Christabel," Seff continued. "But it's the whole chivalrous bit, isn't it? He finds it hard to be rude to anyone, especially women, and so someone like Christabel can ride roughshod over him."

David considered that. Much as he hated to admit it, he had a good idea that Seff might be right. "In any case, it's over now," he said. "Gawaine needn't see her – or any of her little lot – again."

"He'll have to testify at the trial," Seff reminded him. "Unless the police can find enough evidence that they don't have to call him."

"Let's hope they can," David agreed. "You know," he added, sipping his coffee thoughtfully, "this was such an unnecessary murder. Would Father Thomas really have told everyone that Malcolm Braid was transgender? Secrecy of the confessional and all that."

"But Malcolm Braid wasn't *in* the confessional," Seff pointed out. "Father Thomas found it out for himself."

David shrugged. "Whatever. I wouldn't have expected him to spill the beans all over the village."

"But he didn't have to," Seff said. "Once he sacked Malcolm as lay reader – once Malcolm didn't preach that Sunday as scheduled – the gossip would have started. Even if they didn't know the truth, everyone would have known that something was wrong. Rumours would have been flying. One way or the other, Malcolm would have been toast."

"Bad enough for him to panic, I suppose," David said.

"Right. There's nothing wrong with being transgender, but he knew very well how the village would react. And we shouldn't feel too sorry for him," Seff added. "He tried to cover it up, and let the police arrest Richard Coates. And he may not have put the bag over his sister's head, but he was responsible for her death. He deserves what's coming to him."

On that note, she drained her coffee and stood up. "I have to be going. Say hi to Gawaine for me."

"He'll be sorry to have missed you," David said. He had been on the point of asking Seff if she wanted to stay and share a takeaway, and suppressed a sigh of relief at his narrow escape. "He'll probably phone you," he added as he escorted Seff to the door.

"And I'm sure I'll be seeing you again, soon enough," Seff responded. "With Gawaine, there's always a next time."